AF491593

METAL SCAVENGER

PRANAV NATH G

Copyright © Pranav nath G
All Rights Reserved.

This book has been self-published with all reasonable efforts taken to make the material error-free by the author. No part of this book shall be used, reproduced in any manner whatsoever without written permission from the author, except in the case of brief quotations embodied in critical articles and reviews.

The Author of this book is solely responsible and liable for its content including but not limited to the views, representations, descriptions, statements, information, opinions and references ["Content"]. The Content of this book shall not constitute or be construed or deemed to reflect the opinion or expression of the Publisher or Editor. Neither the Publisher nor Editor endorse or approve the Content of this book or guarantee the reliability, accuracy or completeness of the Content published herein and do not make any representations or warranties of any kind, express or implied, including but not limited to the implied warranties of merchantability, fitness for a particular purpose. The Publisher and Editor shall not be liable whatsoever for any errors, omissions, whether such errors or omissions result from negligence, accident, or any other cause or claims for loss or damages of any kind, including without limitation, indirect or consequential loss or damage arising out of use, inability to use, or about the reliability, accuracy or sufficiency of the information contained in this book.

Made with ❤ on the Notion Press Platform
www.notionpress.com

This book is dedicated to my wife Devi Shree, whose unwavering support and belief in me sparked the courage to write. Your constant motivation and the way you saw my potential are the reasons this story exists.

Contents

CHAPTER ONE

Survival in the Margins

Arjun, a boy no older than Eighteen, lived on the very edges of society—on a roadside slum where the world's noise and dust never seemed to rest. His name was rarely spoken beyond his family, and his presence was as unnoticed as the scraps of iron he spent his days collecting. Every morning, as the clock in the nearby temple struck seven, people starts to go to office and children to schools, Arjun stepped onto the broken pavements with a magnet tied to the end of a stick and a burlap sack slung over his thin shoulder.

He would drag the magnet along the roadside with a quiet persistence, letting the dust conceal his bare feet, waiting for the faint click when a nail, a rusted screw, or a shaving of iron clung to the magnet's surface. Each small particle, invisible to passersby, meant survival to him. He bent low, often crawling through piles of garbage, to scrape away the filings that glimmered faintly in the morning sun. His movements were steady, mechanical, almost ritualistic—an unbroken rhythm of scavenging that shaped his young existence.

Arjun was the youngest in a poor family that had no permanent shelter. At night, he lay curled on the roadside under the weak shade of a billboard, using his sack as a pillow, staring at the endless parade of headlights. Any stagnant pond served as his bathroom, and the water, green and oily, doubled as his bath when the grime on his skin began to burn and itch. His elder sister had already left, married off to a man as poor as themselves, in another town far away. His father, who had once introduced him to this practice of scavenging, had long since disappeared into the shadows of his own struggles, leaving Arjun with only the advice to "search where people drop the most."

He remembered those words each time he roamed the city, dragging his magnet stick across markets and streets crowded with footsteps. Yet, it was not until one morning, while passing a narrow lane of small lathe workshops, that his eyes opened to a better truth. As his magnet scraped along the dusty ground, it suddenly bristled with a thick layer of iron dust and shavings. Arjun stopped, staring wide-eyed at the stick. The filings clung so tightly it looked as though the magnet had grown a dark beard overnight.

That moment was his discovery. Without anyone's guidance, without a single hand pointing him toward opportunity, Arjun had realized something important—that the industrial lanes offered him more in minutes than the streets could in hours. It was not luck; it was his own effort, his willingness to test, to search, to observe. He had, unknowingly, conducted his first experiment in survival.

By eight-thirty, his sack was often half-filled. He had learned to finish before the workers poured into the factories at nine-thirty, when the lanes would be crowded and suspicious eyes would follow him. No one knew he existed there—not the workers, not the owners, not even the city that thrived on those very factories. He was invisible, a shadow with a magnet.

For Arjun, this was more than routine; it was instinctive business sense born from necessity. He had discovered a principle that merchants and traders spoke of in polished offices: find the right ground, and you will find wealth. Except Arjun's wealth was measured not in notes or coins, but in fistfuls of black dust that clung to his sack.

The dust itself told stories—tiny fragments that fell when workers moved sheets of metal, when machines spat out sparks, when scraps were shifted from one pile to another. The roads around the factories shimmered faintly with it, as though the city shed its skin in fine metallic flakes.

One morning, a watchman stopped him. The man squinted at Arjun suspiciously, for the guy, covered in black grease from head to toe, looked less like a child and more like a thief caught in the act. His shirt was torn beyond repair, his shorts little more than rags. "What are you doing here?" the watchman demanded, his eyes narrowing.

Arjun clutched his sack nervously but said nothing. To the world, he was only a dirty guy, his face streaked with sweat and dust, his hands blackened by iron. Yet beneath the grime, there was a certain sharpness in his eyes, and had he bathed regularly, the same face might even have been called handsome. But beauty had no place in his life—survival did.

At day's end, the collected metal would be sold to junkyards, where men with sharp eyes and fat ledgers weighed the dust and tossed a few coins into his hand. It was a cruel irony—what was pocket change for them was lifeblood for Arjun. The junkyard owners grew rich off mountains of scrap; Arjun survived off handfuls of filings.

The industrial lane became his kingdom, a place he had cleverly claimed without permission. He had turned the overlooked into opportunity, transforming the scattered dust of factories into the fragile threads that kept him alive.

CHAPTER TWO

The Girl Behind the Wall

The morning arrived like all the others before it—colorless, dusty, and indifferent. Arjun walked his familiar route through the industrial lanes, his magnet stick scraping rhythmically against the ground, collecting the dark offerings the factories unknowingly left behind. The sun had barely risen, and already the air tasted metallic, thick with the residue of welding torches and grinding wheels that would hum to life within the hour.

He moved with the efficiency of someone who had done this a thousand times. Bend, scrape, collect. The filings clung to his magnet in satisfying clumps, and he transferred them carefully into his sack, his fingers blackened and calloused from years of this work. At eighteen, Arjun had perfected his craft. He knew which corners held the richest deposits, which factories discarded the most, and exactly when to disappear before the workers arrived and questions began.

But that morning, something pulled his attention away from the ground.

A movement—slight, cautious—caught the edge of his vision. He looked up and saw her: a young girl, perhaps sixteen or seventeen, standing behind a broken wall near the end of the lane. The wall itself was a remnant of some abandoned construction, its bricks crumbling and covered in faded advertisements and graffiti. She stood in the shadow it cast, her figure partially concealed, as though she belonged to the ruins themselves.

Her clothes were simple, worn but clean—a faded cotton salwar that had seen better days, patched at the knees. Her dupatta, pale blue and threadbare, was wrapped loosely around her shoulders. But it was her eyes that struck him. Wide, dark, and luminous, they followed his every movement with an intensity that was both fearful and curious, like a sparrow watching a cat from a safe distance.

Arjun felt the weight of her gaze and paused mid-motion, his magnet stick hanging in the air. For several seconds, neither of them moved. The city around them continued its awakening—distant horns, the clatter of shutters being raised, the bark of a stray dog—but in that narrow lane, time seemed to hold its breath.

Curiosity overcame caution. Arjun straightened, brushed the worst of the dust from his hands onto his already filthy trousers, and walked toward her. As he approached, she stiffened, her body tensing as though she might bolt at any moment. But she didn't run. She stood her ground, her fingers gripping the edge of the broken wall.

"What are you doing here?" he asked, his voice rougher than he intended, still unused to morning conversation.

The girl flinched slightly at the directness of his question. She looked down at her feet, then back up at him, her expression uncertain. When she finally spoke, her voice was soft, almost a whisper, as though she feared the sound of it might shatter something fragile between them.

"Just watching you," she said. Then, with a hesitance that made her seem even younger, she added, "What are you doing?"

The question was so innocent, so genuine, that Arjun found himself momentarily at a loss. No one had ever asked him that before. To the world, he was invisible—a shadow moving through the margins, unworthy of curiosity or conversation. The workers ignored him. The shopkeepers shooed him away. Even the junkyard owners barely looked at him when they weighed his sack and tossed him his coins.

But this girl—this stranger—had been watching him. And she wanted to know.

He opened his mouth to answer, then closed it again. Something about her gentle tone and the softness in her eyes caught him off guard, made him aware of himself in a way he hadn't been in years. He became suddenly conscious of the grime that covered him from head to toe, the stench of sweat and metal that clung to his skin, the holes in his shirt that revealed patches of his dark, dust-streaked chest. For the first time in a long while, shame flickered through him—not shame of his work, but shame that someone so clean, so delicate, had seen him like this.

Without another word, he turned away and walked back to his magnet stick, resuming his work with a focused intensity that was meant to shut out the world. But he could still feel her eyes on him, watching, and the image of her face—those wide, searching eyes, that gentle voice—lingered in his mind like a song half-remembered.

The next morning, she was there again.

Arjun had told himself he wouldn't look for her, that it didn't matter whether she appeared or not. But the moment he turned into the lane, his eyes instinctively searched the shadows near the broken wall. And there she was, standing in the exact same spot, as though she had never left.

This time, she didn't hide. She stood openly, her hands folded in front of her, watching him with the same quiet curiosity. Arjun felt his heart quicken, though he couldn't say why. He forced himself to focus on his work, dragging his magnet along the ground with deliberate slowness, aware of every movement he made.

By the time he had worked his way down the lane, his sack was heavier than usual. The factories had been busy the day before, and the iron filings lay thick on the ground, clinging to his magnet in dense, bristling layers. The weight of the sack began to slow him down, and he realized he still had another hour of work ahead of him before the workers arrived.

An idea formed in his mind—impulsive, perhaps foolish, but impossible to resist.

He walked toward the girl, the sack slung over his shoulder, its weight pulling at his frame. She straightened as he approached, her expression shifting from curiosity to mild alarm. He stopped a few feet away from her, close enough to see the faint dusting of freckles across her nose, the way her hands trembled slightly at her sides.

"Can I leave this bag here for a while?" he asked, his voice quieter now, almost tentative.

She blinked, surprised by the request. For a moment, she said nothing, her eyes searching his face as though trying to determine whether he could be trusted. Then, without a word, she nodded.

Arjun let out a breath he hadn't realized he'd been holding. He set the heavy sack down gently near the base of the wall, then turned and walked away with his empty, lighter sack, ready to continue his route. As he moved down the lane, he glanced back once and saw her standing beside the bag, her hand resting lightly on its rough surface, as though guarding a treasure.

Something unspoken had shifted between them.

The next day, the same thing happened. And the day after that.

It became their routine, silent and unquestioned. Each morning, Arjun would arrive at the lane, and she would be waiting. He would work until his sack grew heavy, then bring it to her without a word. She would nod, and he would leave it in her care, returning later to collect it before heading to the junkyard.

They spoke little. Sometimes he would ask, "Same place?" and she would nod. Other times, she would simply meet his eyes, and that was enough. But in those small exchanges, something grew—something fragile and nameless, built on trust and silence.

Arjun found himself thinking about her at odd moments throughout the day. While selling his iron at the junkyard, while eating his meager meal of rice and pickle by the roadside, while lying beneath the billboard at night. He wondered who she was, where she came from, why she spent her mornings in that abandoned lane. Was she like him—alone, struggling, surviving on the edges of the world? Or was she something else entirely, something he could never touch?

He didn't know her name. He didn't know her story. But for the first time in his life, Arjun felt something beyond the relentless weight of survival. He felt the stirring of something softer, something that made the gray mornings seem a little less bleak.

And though he didn't yet have the words for it, he knew that the girl behind the wall had become more than a stranger.

She had become a reason to return.

CHAPTER THREE

A Name in the Dust

For nearly two weeks, their routine continued in comfortable silence. Arjun would arrive at dawn, work his route until his sack grew heavy, then leave it with the girl by the broken wall. She would guard it without question, and he would return to collect it before heading to the junkyard. They had become part of each other's mornings, yet they remained strangers—two people orbiting around an unspoken understanding, held together by nothing more than trust and proximity.

But silence, Arjun was learning, had its limits.

The question had been building inside him for days, growing heavier than any sack of iron he carried. Who was she? Why did she come here every morning? What kept her rooted to that spot behind the broken wall, waiting for him as though she had nowhere else to be? The curiosity gnawed at him during his work, distracted him during his meals, and followed him into his restless sleep beneath the billboard.

On the fifteenth morning, he decided he could bear it no longer.

The day began like all the others. The sky was the color of old cement, and the air carried the familiar taste of metal and diesel. Arjun walked his route with his magnet stick, collecting the dark filings that glittered faintly in the early light. His movements were automatic now, his mind elsewhere, rehearsing words he wasn't sure he had the courage to speak.

When he reached the broken wall, she was already there. Meera—though he didn't yet know her name—stood in her usual spot, her pale blue dupatta wrapped around her shoulders against the morning chill. She looked up as he approached, and for a moment, their eyes met. There was something different in her gaze today, something expectant, as though she too had been waiting for this silence to break.

Arjun set down his heavy sack near the base of the wall, but instead of turning away as he always did, he remained standing there. His heart hammered in his chest, and his palms, already blackened with iron dust, grew damp with nervous sweat.

"Can I ask you something?" he said, his voice rougher than he intended.

She tilted her head slightly, surprised but not alarmed. "Yes," she said softly.

He hesitated, suddenly aware of how simple the question was, yet how much it meant to him. "What's your name?"

For a long moment, she didn't answer. She looked down at her hands, then back up at him, and something flickered across her face—uncertainty, perhaps, or the same kind of nervousness he felt. When she finally spoke, her voice was barely above a whisper.

"Meera."

The name settled between them like something fragile and precious. Arjun repeated it silently in his mind, tasting the shape of it, committing it to memory. Meera. It suited her—soft, gentle, with a quiet strength beneath its simplicity.

"Meera," he said aloud, testing the sound of it on his tongue. A small smile touched the corners of her lips, so brief he almost missed it.

"And you?" she asked, her voice gaining a bit more confidence. "What's your name?"

"Arjun."

She nodded slowly, as though filing the name away somewhere safe. "Arjun," she repeated, and hearing his name spoken in her voice did something strange to him—made him feel seen in a way he hadn't felt in years. Not as a shadow, not as a scavenger, but as a person with a name worth remembering.

They stood there for a moment, neither quite knowing what to say next. The city around them continued its morning awakening—the distant rumble of trucks, the clang of metal gates being raised, the call of a street vendor somewhere far off. But in that narrow lane, with only the broken wall and the iron dust as witnesses, something had shifted between them.

"Why do you come here every morning?" Arjun asked, the question spilling out before he could stop himself. "I mean... you don't have to. You could be anywhere else."

Meera looked away, her gaze drifting toward the end of the lane where the factories stood like silent giants. When she spoke, her voice was quieter, tinged with something he couldn't quite name—sadness, perhaps, or resignation.

"I live nearby," she said. "With my uncle and his family. I... I don't have much to do in the mornings. They don't need me until later, so I come here." She paused, then added, almost shyly, "I noticed you one day, working so hard, so early. I was curious. No one else seemed to see you, but I did."

The admission struck him with unexpected force. No one else seemed to see you, but I did. Those simple words carried a weight that made his chest tighten. For so long, invisibility had been his shield, his protection against a world that had no use for people like him. But she had seen him. And instead of looking away, she had kept watching.

"Why do you do this?" Meera asked, gesturing toward the sack of iron at their feet. "Collecting... this?"

Arjun looked down at his blackened hands, at the stick with the magnet still clutched in his grip. How could he explain a life she had probably never known? How could he put into words the brutal mathematics of survival—that each handful of iron meant food, that each sack meant another day, that stopping meant disappearing entirely?

"It's how I live," he said simply. "I collect iron filings from the factories and sell them to junkyards. It's not much, but it's enough. Barely."

She was silent for a moment, absorbing this. Then she asked, so quietly he almost didn't hear, "Do you have family?"

The question was a knife, sharp and unexpected. Arjun looked away, his jaw tightening. "I did. My father... he left a long time ago. My sister got married and moved away. It's just me now."

"I'm sorry," Meera said, and the sincerity in her voice made him look back at her. There was no pity in her eyes, only understanding—the kind that came from someone who knew what it meant to be alone.

"What about you?" he asked. "Your uncle—is he good to you?"

Meera's expression flickered, something unreadable passing across her face. "He gave me a place to stay after my parents died," she said carefully. "That's more than I had. But..." She trailed off, leaving the rest unspoken, and Arjun understood. Some kindnesses came with invisible chains.

They fell into silence again, but it was different now—not the silence of strangers, but the silence of two people who had shared something real. Arjun felt the urge to say more, to ask more, but he didn't want to push too hard, too fast. This fragile connection between them felt precious, and he was terrified of breaking it.

"I should go," he said reluctantly, glancing toward the lane where his work awaited. "There's more to collect before the workers arrive."

Meera nodded, but she didn't step back. "Will you... will you come back tomorrow?" she asked, and there was something in her voice—hope, perhaps, or fear that he might not.

"Yes," Arjun said without hesitation. "I'll come back."

A genuine smile broke across her face then, small but radiant, and it transformed her entirely. For a brief moment, she didn't look like someone burdened by loss or circumstance. She looked like a girl who had found something worth smiling about.

Arjun turned and walked away, his empty sack slung over his shoulder, but he couldn't stop himself from glancing back once. She was still standing there, watching him go, her hand resting lightly on the sack he had left in her care.

And for the first time in years, as he dragged his magnet along the dusty ground, Arjun felt something unfamiliar blooming in his chest—not just the grim determination to survive another day, but the quiet joy of knowing that someone, somewhere, was waiting for him to return.

Her name was Meera. And now she knew his was Arjun.

It was a small thing, perhaps. Just two names exchanged in the dust and the dawn. But to him, it felt like the beginning of something he couldn't yet name—something that made the iron filings seem lighter, the morning sky seem brighter, and the weight of his solitary existence seem just a little more bearable.

That evening, at the junkyard, the owner weighed Arjun's sack and tossed him his usual coins without a word. But as Arjun walked away, clutching the meager payment in his blackened hand, he realized something had changed.

The coins felt the same. The work felt the same. But he no longer felt the same.

Somewhere in the margins of the city, in a narrow lane behind a broken wall, someone knew his name. And that, somehow, made all the difference.

CHAPTER FOUR

Small Acts of Kindness

The days that followed the exchange of names felt different to Arjun, as though the world had subtly rearranged itself around him. The factories still rumbled to life at the same hour. The iron filings still clung to his magnet with the same metallic whisper. The sun still rose over the same dusty lanes. But now, woven into the fabric of his morning routine, was the quiet anticipation of seeing Meera.

She was always there when he arrived, standing by the broken wall as though she had been waiting for hours. And perhaps she had been. Arjun never asked, afraid that knowing might make him feel guilty for the hope he saw in her eyes each time he turned the corner into their lane.

Their conversations grew longer, more frequent. What had begun as a simple exchange of names expanded slowly, carefully, like a plant pushing through concrete. They spoke in fragments at first—small observations about the weather, the noise of the factories, the stray dogs that wandered the lanes. But gradually, the fragments became fuller, richer, until their mornings were filled with more than just the sound of his magnet scraping against the ground.

It was on a Tuesday morning, nearly three weeks after they had first spoken, that Meera brought him water.

Arjun had been working longer than usual that day. The factories had been busy over the weekend, and the ground was littered with more iron filings than he had seen in months. His sack was already half-full, and he was drenched in sweat, his throat parched and raw from the dust that hung perpetually in the air.

When he approached the broken wall to leave his sack with Meera, she was holding something—a small steel tumbler, scratched and dented but clean. She extended it toward him without a word, her eyes searching his face with a mixture of shyness and concern.

"I thought you might be thirsty," she said quietly.

Arjun stared at the tumbler, then at her, unable to move. For a moment, he didn't know what to do. No one had offered him water in years—not freely, not with kindness. At the tea stalls, he had to pay. At the public taps, he had to fight for his turn. But here was Meera, holding out something as simple as water as though it were the most natural thing in the world.

"I..." he started, his voice catching. He cleared his throat and tried again. "Thank you."

He took the tumbler from her, their fingers brushing for the briefest moment—hers soft and clean, his rough and blackened with iron dust. The contrast made him acutely aware of the space between their worlds, yet she didn't pull away. She simply watched as he lifted the tumbler to his lips and drank.

The water was cool, slightly sweet, and tasted faintly of the steel container. It was the best thing Arjun had tasted in weeks. He drank slowly, savoring each sip, feeling the liquid soothe his parched throat and settle the dust in his lungs. When he finished, he handed the tumbler back to her, reluctant to let go of the small comfort it represented.

"Thank you," he said again, more earnestly this time.

Meera smiled, a genuine smile that reached her eyes and made something in his chest tighten. "You work so hard," she said. "I can see how tired you get. It's the least I could do."

Arjun wanted to tell her that it wasn't the least—that it was everything. That in a world where he was invisible, ignored, and dismissed, this simple act of noticing his thirst felt like a miracle. But the words stuck in his throat, tangled with emotions he didn't know how to name.

Instead, he said, "I'll bring the tumbler back tomorrow. Clean."

"You don't have to—"

"I want to," he interrupted, his voice firmer than he intended. "Please."

She nodded, understanding something unspoken in his insistence. It wasn't just about returning a borrowed item. It was about reciprocity, about proving that he wasn't just someone who took without giving, that he had dignity even if he had nothing else.

The next morning, Arjun arrived earlier than usual. He had spent the previous evening scrubbing the tumbler with sand and water from a public tap, polishing it until it gleamed as much as its battered surface would allow. When he handed it back to Meera, he saw the surprise in her eyes—not at its cleanliness, but at the care he had taken.

"Thank you," she said, accepting it with a small smile. Then, almost shyly, she added, "I brought it again today. If you want."

And so it became part of their routine. Each morning, Meera would bring him water, and each morning, Arjun would drink it gratefully, wash the tumbler at the end of his work, and return it to her the next day. It was a small ritual, but it bound them together in a way that words could not.

A week later, Arjun decided to reciprocate in his own way.

He had sold a particularly good haul of iron filings and, for once, had a few extra coins jangling in his pocket. Instead of saving them or spending them on food, he stopped at a small roadside stall on his way back from the junkyard and bought something he hadn't purchased in years—a packet of roasted peanuts, still warm and fragrant with salt and spice.

The next morning, when he arrived at the broken wall, he pulled the packet from his pocket and held it out to Meera.

"For you," he said, suddenly feeling self-conscious. "I thought... I thought you might like them."

Meera's eyes widened in surprise. She looked at the packet, then at him, and for a moment, he worried he had made a mistake—that she would find his offering too simple, too cheap, too much like the scraps he lived on.

But then she took the packet from him, her fingers closing gently around it, and smiled. "Thank you, Arjun," she said, and the way she said his name—with warmth and something that sounded almost like affection—made his heart skip.

She opened the packet and offered it back to him. "Share with me?"

He hesitated, then took a small handful. They stood there together in the early morning light, eating roasted peanuts in companionable silence, and Arjun realized that this—this simple act of sharing—felt more intimate than anything he had ever experienced.

As the days passed, their conversations deepened. They talked about small things—the colors of the sky at dawn, the sounds of the city waking up, the patterns of the seasons. But they also talked about bigger things, though always carefully, as though testing the boundaries of what they could share.

Meera told him about the books she had once read before her parents died, about the stories that still lived in her memory. Arjun, who had never learned to read beyond recognizing numbers and a few basic signs, listened with fascination as she described worlds he could never enter.

"I wish I could read," he admitted one morning, the confession slipping out before he could stop it.

Meera looked at him thoughtfully. "I could teach you," she said. "If you want. I don't have any books here, but I could write in the dust. Simple words at first."

The offer stunned him. "You would do that?"

"Of course," she said, as though it were obvious. "You've been kind to me, Arjun. Let me be kind to you."

And so, another ritual was added to their mornings. After Arjun left his sack with her and before he went back to work, Meera would crouch down and use a stick to write letters in the dust. She started with his name—A-R-J-U-N—tracing each letter carefully and making him repeat the sounds until he could recognize them. Then she wrote her own name—M-E-E-R-A—and watched as he slowly, painstakingly, traced the letters with his finger.

It was slow, frustrating work. His hands, calloused and clumsy from years of physical labor, struggled to form the delicate shapes. But Meera was patient, encouraging, never mocking or dismissive. And gradually, letter by letter, word by word, Arjun began to see the world differently—not just as a place of surfaces and things, but as a place of meanings and messages.

One morning, nearly a month after they had exchanged names, Arjun arrived to find Meera sitting on a small cloth she had spread on the ground near the broken wall. She looked up as he approached, and there was something different in her expression—something lighter, almost playful.

"I brought something today," she said, reaching into a small cloth bag beside her. She pulled out two small bananas, slightly overripe but still good. "I thought we could have breakfast together. If you have time."

Arjun looked at the bananas, then at her, and felt something shift in his chest—a warmth that had nothing to do with the rising sun. She had brought food for him. She wanted to share a meal with him. Not out of pity, but because she wanted his company.

"I have time," he said, his voice rough with emotion he couldn't quite hide.

He sat down across from her on the dusty ground, conscious of the grime that covered him, of the smell of sweat and metal that clung to his clothes. But Meera didn't seem to notice or care. She handed him a banana and peeled her own, and they ate together in the quiet morning, the city slowly coming alive around them.

"Do you ever think about the future?" Meera asked suddenly, her voice soft and contemplative.

Arjun paused mid-bite, caught off guard by the question. The future? For most of his life, the future had been nothing more than the next day, the next meal, the next sack of iron to fill. But lately, since meeting Meera, he had found himself thinking about things he had never dared to imagine before—stability, comfort, perhaps even happiness.

"Sometimes," he admitted. "But it's hard to think beyond tomorrow when today is already so difficult."

Meera nodded, her gaze distant. "I understand," she said. "But sometimes I let myself imagine. What it would be like to have choices. To not feel... trapped."

The word hung in the air between them—trapped. Arjun understood it intimately. He was trapped by poverty, by circumstance, by the relentless need to survive. And Meera, he was beginning to realize, was trapped in her own way—by obligation, by dependence, by the invisible chains of a life lived at someone else's mercy.

"Maybe one day," he said quietly, "we'll both have choices."

Meera looked at him then, really looked at him, and in her eyes he saw something that made his breath catch—hope, fragile and tentative, but undeniably there.

"Maybe," she whispered.

They finished their bananas in silence, but it was a comfortable silence, heavy with unspoken understanding. When Arjun stood to resume his work, Meera stood too, brushing the dust from her clothes.

"Same time tomorrow?" she asked, though by now it was more ritual than question.

"Same time tomorrow," he confirmed.

As he walked away, his magnet stick in hand and his empty sack over his shoulder, Arjun realized that something fundamental had changed. Meera was no longer just the girl who guarded his sack or brought him water. She was becoming something more—something precious, something he couldn't afford to lose.

And though he didn't say it aloud, didn't even fully acknowledge it to himself, he knew that what he felt for her was no longer just gratitude or friendship.

It was the beginning of love.

That evening, as Arjun lay beneath his billboard, staring up at the stars that barely pierced through the city's haze, he allowed himself to imagine a different life. A life where he wasn't covered in iron dust. A life where he had a home, a future, something to offer someone like Meera.

It was a dangerous dream, he knew. Dreams required hope, and hope required the belief that change was possible. For someone like him, born and raised in the margins, such beliefs felt like luxuries he couldn't afford.

But as he closed his eyes and the image of Meera's smile filled his mind, he decided that maybe—just maybe—some luxuries were worth reaching for, even if they remained forever out of grasp.

Because now he had something he hadn't had before: a reason to want more than mere survival.

He had Meera.

CHAPTER FIVE

The Weight of Obligation

Meera had not always lived in the narrow house at the end of the lane, with its peeling paint and perpetually damp walls. There had been a time, though it felt like a lifetime ago, when she had lived in a small but sunlit apartment with her parents—a time when her mother's laughter filled the rooms and her father returned home each evening with stories from his work at the textile mill.

But that time had ended abruptly three years ago, when a faulty electrical wire had sparked a fire in their building. Her parents had perished in the smoke and flames, and Meera, who had been visiting a neighbor that evening, had returned to find everything she had ever known reduced to ash and memory.

She had been fifteen then, alone and terrified, with no siblings and no other relatives except her mother's younger brother—Uncle Ramesh—who lived on the outskirts of the city with his wife and two young sons. He had come to the hospital where Meera sat wrapped in a borrowed shawl, her eyes hollow with shock, and had offered her what he called "a home."

"You're family," he had said, though his voice carried more duty than warmth. "We'll take care of you."

And so Meera had moved into the small house with the crumbling courtyard and the narrow rooms that always smelled faintly of cooking oil and damp concrete. Uncle Ramesh worked as a supervisor at a mid-sized factory—not wealthy, but comfortable enough to afford three meals a day and school fees for his sons. His wife, Aunt Lakshmi, was a sharp-tongued woman whose kindness came with conditions and whose hospitality was measured in obligations.

From the beginning, it was made clear to Meera that she was not a daughter in this house. She was a ward, a responsibility, someone to be fed and sheltered in exchange for usefulness.

Meera's days followed a rigid pattern. She woke before dawn to prepare breakfast for the family—strong tea with too much sugar for Uncle Ramesh, milk and biscuits for her two young cousins, and plain tea with yesterday's rice for Aunt Lakshmi, who was always watching her weight but never successfully. By the time the family sat down to eat, Meera had already swept the courtyard, washed the previous night's dishes, and drawn water from the public tap two streets away.

After breakfast, she would get her cousins ready for school—combing their hair, checking their homework, packing their lunch boxes with parathas and pickle. Aunt Lakshmi, who slept late and rose slowly, would supervise from the doorway, offering corrections and criticisms in equal measure.

"The tea is too weak today, Meera."

"You've burned the edges of the paratha again."

"Can't you tie his shoelaces properly? What use are you if you can't even do that?"

Meera absorbed these comments in silence, nodding and murmuring apologies, her face carefully neutral. Resistance, she had learned early, only made things worse. Aunt Lakshmi's tongue could be as sharp as a blade when provoked, and Uncle Ramesh, though not unkind, would always side with his wife.

Once the children left for school and Uncle Ramesh departed for the factory, the house would settle into a tense quiet. Aunt Lakshmi would retreat to her room to watch television or gossip with neighbors, leaving Meera to complete the endless list of chores—washing clothes by hand, scrubbing floors, chopping vegetables for the evening meal, mending torn clothes, cleaning the bathroom that always seemed to accumulate grime faster than she could remove it.

By mid-morning, when the worst of the work was done and Aunt Lakshmi was occupied, Meera would slip out of the house. She told herself it was to buy vegetables from the market or to fetch something her aunt had forgotten. But the truth was simpler and more desperate: she needed to breathe.

That was how she had first found the lane with the broken wall. It was on her way to nowhere in particular, a detour she had taken one morning to avoid a neighbor who asked too many questions. The lane was quiet, industrial, forgotten by most people. And in that quietness, Meera had found a brief sanctuary—a place where no one told her what to do, where no one expected anything from her, where she could simply exist without apology.

And then, one morning, she had seen Arjun.

At first, he had been just another figure in the landscape—a boy covered in dust, dragging a magnet along the ground with the focus of someone who had no choice but to work. But something about him had captured her attention. Perhaps it was the quiet determination in his movements, or the way he worked alone without complaint, or simply the fact that he, like her, seemed to exist on the margins of a world that had no use for people like them.

She had watched him for days before he noticed her, and in those days of watching, she had begun to look forward to the mornings in a way she hadn't in years. Seeing Arjun became the one part of her day that belonged entirely to her—a secret pocket of time that Aunt Lakshmi couldn't claim, that her cousins couldn't interrupt, that Uncle Ramesh's disapproving silences couldn't taint.

When Arjun had finally spoken to her, when he had asked her name and she had answered, something inside her had shifted. For the first time since her parents' death, someone had seen her not as an obligation or a servant, but as a person worth knowing.

But the freedom Meera found in those morning hours came at a cost.

One morning, after she had been meeting Arjun for nearly a month, she returned home later than usual. The teaching session—where she had been showing Arjun how to write simple words in the dust—had run long, and by the time she slipped back into the house, Aunt Lakshmi was already awake and waiting.

"Where have you been?" her aunt demanded, her arms crossed over her chest, her eyes hard and suspicious.

"The vegetable market," Meera lied smoothly, holding up the small bag of tomatoes and onions she had hastily purchased on her way back. "The vendor near the house didn't have fresh vegetables, so I went to the one by the main road."

Aunt Lakshmi's eyes narrowed. "You were gone for over an hour. It doesn't take that long to buy vegetables."

"There was a queue," Meera said, keeping her voice steady. "Many people were—"

"Don't lie to me," Aunt Lakshmi snapped, stepping closer. "You think I don't know what girls your age get up to when they're left unsupervised? Wandering around, talking to boys, ruining their reputation and ours?"

Meera's heart hammered in her chest, but she kept her expression carefully blank. "I wasn't doing anything wrong, Aunt. I was just—"

"You were just taking advantage of our kindness," Aunt Lakshmi interrupted, her voice rising. "We took you in when you had nothing, gave you food and shelter, and this is how you repay us? By sneaking around like some common—"

"Lakshmi, enough."

Uncle Ramesh's voice cut through the room, firm but not loud. He stood in the doorway, having just returned from his morning walk, his face weary and resigned. He looked at Meera, then at his wife, and sighed.

"The girl went to buy vegetables," he said quietly. "Let her be."

Aunt Lakshmi opened her mouth to protest, but something in her husband's tone made her reconsider. She huffed, shooting Meera a look that promised the conversation was far from over, and stalked off to the kitchen.

Uncle Ramesh remained in the doorway for a moment, his gaze resting on Meera with an expression she couldn't quite read. "Don't give her reasons to doubt you," he said softly. "We've done what we could for you. Don't make us regret it."

The words, spoken without malice but heavy with implication, struck Meera like a physical blow. Don't make us regret it. As though her very existence in this house was a favor that could be revoked at any moment.

"I won't, Uncle," she whispered, her throat tight.

He nodded once and left, and Meera stood alone in the dim hallway, the bag of vegetables clutched in her trembling hands.

That evening, as she chopped onions for dinner, her eyes stinging from both the onions and unshed tears, Meera thought about Arjun. She thought about the way he looked at her—not with suspicion or expectation, but with kindness and something that felt dangerously close to admiration. She thought about the mornings they spent together, the simple rituals they had built, the way his presence made her feel like more than just a burden someone had agreed to carry.

In Arjun's eyes, she was Meera. Not the orphaned niece. Not the unpaid servant. Not the girl who should be grateful for every scrap of tolerance thrown her way.

Just Meera.

And that, she realized, was why she kept going back to the lane with the broken wall, even knowing the risks. Because those mornings with Arjun were the only time she felt like herself—the only time she felt seen in a way that didn't make her feel small.

The next morning, Meera arrived at the lane earlier than usual, her heart still heavy from the confrontation with Aunt Lakshmi. When Arjun appeared, his face lit up in that way it always did when he saw her, and something in her chest loosened.

"Good morning," he said, his voice warm despite the early hour and the dust that already clung to his clothes.

"Good morning," she replied, managing a small smile.

They fell into their usual routine—Arjun leaving his sack with her, the two of them sharing a few words before he returned to work. But today, Arjun seemed to sense something different in her mood. He hesitated before turning to leave, his dark eyes searching her face.

"Are you all right?" he asked quietly.

The question, so simple and sincere, nearly undid her. When was the last time someone had asked her that? When was the last time anyone had cared about the answer?

"I'm fine," she lied, because the truth was too complicated, too painful to put into words.

But Arjun didn't look convinced. He took a step closer, his expression serious. "If something's wrong... if you ever need help, or just someone to talk to... I'm here."

The words were awkward, unpracticed, as though he wasn't used to offering comfort. But that only made them more precious. Meera felt tears prick at the corners of her eyes, and she blinked them back quickly, not wanting him to see.

"Thank you," she whispered. "That means more than you know."

Arjun nodded, still watching her with concern, but he didn't push. He simply gave her a small, reassuring smile and walked away to continue his work.

As Meera watched him go, she made a silent promise to herself. No matter what Aunt Lakshmi said, no matter how suspicious her uncle became, she would find a way to keep coming here. These mornings with Arjun were the only good thing in her life, and she wasn't ready to give them up.

Not yet.

Not ever, if she could help it.

But even as she made that promise, a small voice in the back of her mind whispered a warning: How long can you keep this secret? And what will happen when they find out?

Meera pushed the thought away, unwilling to face it. For now, she had this morning, this moment, this fragile connection with someone who saw her as more than an obligation.

For now, that would have to be enough.

CHAPTER SIX

The Seed of Ambition

Arjun had always known that Meera's life was not easy—he could see it in the weariness that sometimes shadowed her eyes, in the way her hands were calloused despite their delicacy, in the careful way she rationed the small pleasures she allowed herself. But it wasn't until one morning, when she arrived with a bruise darkening her forearm, that the full weight of her situation began to reveal itself.

"What happened?" he asked immediately, his voice sharper than he intended, his eyes fixed on the purple-blue mark that stood out starkly against her skin.

Meera glanced down at her arm as though she had forgotten it was there. "It's nothing," she said quickly, pulling her dupatta to cover it. "I just... I bumped into the kitchen door. Clumsy."

But Arjun had lived too long on the streets, had seen too many kinds of hurt, to accept that explanation. The shape of the bruise was too deliberate, too much like fingers pressed hard into flesh. His jaw tightened, and something hot and unfamiliar flared in his chest—anger, protective and fierce.

"Did someone hurt you?" he asked, his voice low.

Meera's eyes widened slightly, and for a moment, he saw fear flicker across her face—not fear of him, but fear of the conversation, of what admitting the truth might mean. She shook her head quickly, too quickly.

"No, Arjun. Really. It was an accident. I was carrying a heavy pot and—"

"Meera."

The single word, spoken with quiet intensity, stopped her. He stepped closer, close enough that he could see the exhaustion etched into her young face, the tension she carried in her shoulders, the careful way she held herself as though braced for the next blow—physical or verbal.

"You don't have to lie to me," he said softly. "I know what it's like to... to live in places where you're not wanted. Where people make you feel like you should be grateful just for existing in their space."

Something in her expression crumbled. Her carefully maintained composure wavered, and for a moment, she looked like she might cry. But she didn't. Instead, she took a shaky breath and looked away, her gaze fixed on some distant point beyond the broken wall.

"My aunt," she whispered finally. "She gets... frustrated sometimes. Yesterday I didn't cook the rice properly. It was too soft. She grabbed my arm when she was scolding me. She didn't mean to hurt me. She just forgets her own strength."

The words came out rehearsed, like a script she had told herself so many times she almost believed it. But Arjun heard what lay beneath them—the excuses, the minimization, the desperate need to make the situation bearable by pretending it was less than it was.

"How often does she forget her strength?" he asked quietly.

Meera's silence was answer enough.

Arjun felt something shift inside him—a rage so pure and helpless it made his hands tremble. He wanted to march to that house, to confront the aunt who treated Meera like property, to pull Meera away from that place and keep her safe. But what could he offer? He lived on the street. He owned nothing but a magnet stick and a burlap sack. He was nobody, nothing, a shadow that the world stepped over without noticing.

The realization crashed over him like cold water: he couldn't protect Meera. He couldn't offer her safety or comfort or even the promise of something better. He was as powerless as she was, trapped in his own kind of prison.

But unlike Meera, his prison had no walls. And that meant, perhaps, that he could find a way out.

That night, lying beneath his billboard as trucks rumbled past and the city hummed its endless song, Arjun made a decision.

He would not remain nothing forever.

For eighteen years, he had accepted his lot without question. Survival had been enough—waking up each day, filling his sack, earning just enough to eat, then doing it all again. He had never asked for more because asking for more seemed like a foolish dream, a luxury reserved for people who had the privilege of choices.

But now he had a reason to want more. He had Meera.

And if he was going to be worthy of her—if he was going to have any chance of offering her something better than bruises and borrowed space in someone else's home—he needed to change. Not just his circumstances, but himself.

He needed to become more.

The next morning, Arjun arrived at the lane with a new determination burning in his chest. When he saw Meera waiting by the broken wall, her bruised arm still hidden beneath her dupatta, his resolve only strengthened.

"I've been thinking," he said after their usual greetings, his voice more serious than she had ever heard it. "About the future."

Meera looked at him curiously. "What about it?"

"I want more than this," he said, gesturing vaguely at himself—at the dust that covered him, at the stick and sack that defined his existence. "I want... I want to be able to offer something. To build something. Not just survive, but actually live."

Something flickered in Meera's eyes—surprise, perhaps, or hope, or fear that hoping might lead to disappointment. "What do you mean?" she asked softly.

"I don't know yet," Arjun admitted. "But I know I can't stay like this forever. Collecting iron filings is... it's kept me alive. But it's not a future. It's just an endless present."

He paused, gathering his courage for what he wanted to say next. "I want to be someone you don't have to hide," he said quietly. "Someone who could... who could take care of you. If you ever needed it."

Meera's breath caught. For a long moment, she simply stared at him, her eyes wide and glistening with unshed tears. Then, very quietly, she said, "You already take care of me, Arjun. Just by being here. Just by seeing me."

"That's not enough," he said, his voice rough with emotion. "You deserve more than someone who can barely feed himself. You deserve safety. Respect. A life where you're not afraid of making the rice too soft."

A single tear slipped down Meera's cheek, and she quickly wiped it away. "And you deserve more than sleeping on streets and scraping metal from the ground," she said. "But wanting and having are different things."

"I know," Arjun said. "But maybe... maybe I can change that. I'm not sure how yet, but I'm going to try."

Over the following days, Arjun's mind became a constant churning of ideas and possibilities. He observed everything with new eyes, looking for opportunities he had previously been too focused on survival to notice.

He watched the factory owners arriving in their cars, the supervisors barking orders, the skilled workers who commanded higher wages. He listened to conversations in the junkyard, learning about prices and demand, about which metals were worth more, about the businesses built on scrap and salvage.

One afternoon, while selling his iron at the junkyard, he struck up a conversation with the owner—a gruff man named Patel who had grown wealthy buying low and selling high.

"Why do you pay so little for iron filings?" Arjun asked, more boldly than he had ever spoken to the man before.

Patel looked at him with surprise, then amusement. "Because filings are the lowest grade. Mixed with dirt, inconsistent quality. I have to process them, clean them, melt them down. That costs money."

"What if they were cleaner?" Arjun asked. "What if I separated the dirt better, brought you purer metal?"

Patel laughed. "Then I'd pay you more, boy. But that would take time you don't have. You need to fill your sack every day just to eat, don't you?"

It was true. But it also planted a seed in Arjun's mind. What if he could find a way to work smarter, not just harder? What if he could improve the quality of what he collected, or find better sources, or learn skills that would make him more valuable?

That night, instead of sleeping, Arjun lay awake thinking. He thought about the mechanics he had seen in the factories, the welders whose skills commanded respect and steady wages. He thought about the small entrepreneurs who started with nothing and built businesses from scraps and determination.

He thought about education—about the reading and writing Meera was teaching him. It was slow, painfully slow, but already he could recognize more words than he had ever thought possible. What if he learned more? What if he could read contracts, signs, instructions? What if he could present himself as someone literate, capable, worthy of something better than collecting dust?

The path wasn't clear. He had no money for formal education, no connections to help him climb, no safety net if he failed. But for the first time in his life, failure felt less terrifying than never trying. Because now he had something—someone—worth trying for.

The next morning, he told Meera about his conversation with Patel.

"He said he'd pay more for cleaner metal," Arjun explained, his eyes bright with possibility. "So I'm going to find a way to make that happen. Maybe I can sift the filings somehow, separate the dirt. It'll take more time, but if I can earn even a little more..."

"You could save," Meera said, understanding immediately. "Build something."

"Exactly," Arjun said. "It's not much. It's not fast. But it's a start."

Meera smiled then—a genuine, radiant smile that made something in his chest expand. "I think you can do it," she said. "You're clever, Arjun. Cleverer than you give yourself credit for. Look at how you found the factory lanes on your own, how you learned where the best filings were. You have good instincts."

Her faith in him was almost overwhelming. No one had ever believed in him before—not his father, not his sister, not the world that had relegated him to its margins. But Meera believed. And that belief felt like fuel, like oxygen to a flame that had just begun to burn.

"There's something else," he said, hesitating. "The reading lessons you've been giving me. Could we... could we do more of that? I know it takes your time, but if I could read better, write better, maybe I could find better work eventually. Real work."

"Of course," Meera said immediately. "I'll teach you as much as I know. We can practice every morning, for as long as you want."

"Thank you," Arjun said, and the gratitude in his voice went deeper than words could express.

In the days that followed, Arjun threw himself into his new purpose with an intensity that surprised even himself. He began waking even earlier, using the extra time to separate the cleaner filings from the dirt-heavy ones. He experimented with different methods—using a piece of cloth to sift, wetting the filings slightly so the dust would stick together and could be blown away, working more carefully to avoid contamination.

It was painstaking work, and it cut into his collecting time, which meant his sacks were sometimes lighter than before. But when he brought the cleaner metal to Patel, the junkyard owner examined it with raised eyebrows.

"This is better," Patel admitted grudgingly. "Much better."

He paid Arjun twenty percent more than usual—not a fortune, but enough to make the extra effort worthwhile.

Arjun clutched the coins tightly, feeling the weight of them not just as money but as proof. Proof that he could improve, that he could learn, that he could become something more than what circumstances had made him.

That evening, he didn't spend the extra money on food as he normally would have. Instead, he hid it carefully in a cloth tied around his waist—the beginning of his savings, the foundation of whatever future he could build.

Meanwhile, Meera's morning lessons became more intensive. She taught him not just letters but words, then simple sentences. She showed him how to write his own name with confidence, how to read basic signs and notices. She brought scraps of newspaper when she could find them, and they would sit together deciphering the words, Arjun's finger tracing each line as Meera gently corrected his pronunciation.

"You're learning fast," she said one morning, genuine pride in her voice. "Faster than I expected."

"I have a good teacher," Arjun replied, smiling. "And a good reason to learn."

Their eyes met, and something passed between them—an acknowledgment of what was growing between them, unnamed but undeniable. It was more than friendship now, deeper than gratitude. It was the beginning of something that made both their difficult lives feel bearable, even meaningful.

One morning, about two months after Arjun had first decided to change his life, he arrived at the broken wall with something hidden in his hand. He had been saving carefully, spending only on absolute necessities, and finally he had enough for what he wanted to buy.

"I have something for you," he said to Meera, his voice nervous.

He opened his hand to reveal a simple hairclip—nothing fancy, just a small metal clip with a delicate flower design, the kind sold at roadside stalls for a few rupees. But he had chosen it carefully, making sure it was the prettiest one he could afford, polishing it with the edge of his shirt until it shined.

Meera stared at it, her eyes wide. "Arjun..."

"It's not much," he said quickly, embarrassed. "I know it's nothing compared to what you deserve. But I wanted... I wanted to give you something. Something that's just yours, that no one can take away or criticize or make you feel bad about."

Meera's hand trembled as she reached for the hairclip. She held it gently, as though it were made of glass, and when she looked up at him, her eyes were bright with tears.

"It's beautiful," she whispered. "It's the most beautiful thing anyone has ever given me."

She removed her old, worn hairclip—a plain plastic thing that was cracked and faded—and carefully fastened the new one in her hair. The small metal flower caught the morning light, and Arjun thought he had never seen anything more lovely than Meera in that moment, with his gift in her hair and tears of happiness on her cheeks.

"Thank you," she said, her voice breaking slightly. "Thank you, Arjun."

He wanted to tell her that it was nothing, that she deserved so much more, that one day he would give her everything she had ever been denied. But the words stuck in his throat, too big and too fragile to speak aloud.

Instead, he simply said, "One day, Meera. One day I'll be able to give you more than hairclips. I promise."

And in that moment, standing in the dusty lane beside the broken wall, with the city waking around them and the future still uncertain, they both chose to believe that promise was possible.

Because sometimes, belief was all you had. And sometimes, it was enough to start building a different life.

CHAPTER SEVEN

Rising from the Dust

Three months had passed since Arjun had given Meera the hairclip, and in that time, something fundamental had shifted in the trajectory of his life. The change was gradual, almost imperceptible from day to day, but when he looked back at who he had been just a few months ago, the distance felt immense.

He was no longer just surviving. He was building.

The extra income from providing cleaner iron filings had given him breathing room—not wealth, not even comfort, but the smallest margin of financial safety. Instead of spending every rupee immediately on food, he now had a small cloth pouch hidden beneath his sleeping spot under the billboard, and inside that pouch, coins accumulated slowly but steadily.

Fifty rupees. Then a hundred. Then a hundred and fifty.

It was nothing by most standards—barely enough to buy a decent meal at a restaurant—but to Arjun, it represented something revolutionary: the possibility of choice. The possibility of a future that wasn't dictated entirely by the demands of each immediate day.

One morning, while making his rounds through the industrial lanes, Arjun noticed something he had seen hundreds of times before but never truly observed: a small repair shop tucked between two larger factories. The shop specialized in fixing industrial machinery—lathes, grinding wheels, metal presses—and its owner, an elderly man named Rajan, worked alone, his skilled hands moving with the precision of decades of experience.

Arjun had always passed the shop without much thought, but this time he paused, watching as Rajan disassembled a broken lathe motor with practiced efficiency. There was something mesmerizing about the way the old man worked—the confidence, the knowledge, the ability to take something broken and make it whole again.

"What are you staring at, boy?" Rajan called out without looking up, his voice gruff but not unkind.

Arjun startled, embarrassed at being caught. "Sorry, sir. I was just... watching you work."

Rajan finally looked up, squinting at him through oil-smudged glasses. "You're that scavenger kid, aren't you? The one who collects iron filings."

"Yes, sir."

"Hm." Rajan returned his attention to the motor, using a wrench to loosen a stubborn bolt. "Well, don't just stand there. If you're going to watch, make yourself useful. Hand me that smaller wrench on the bench."

Arjun hesitated for only a moment before setting down his stick and sack and stepping into the shop. He found the wrench Rajan had indicated and handed it over carefully.

"Thank you," Rajan muttered, using the tool to reach a bolt that his larger wrench couldn't access. "You have any interest in this kind of work, or are you just killing time?"

The question caught Arjun off guard. Did he have interest? He had never considered it before—had never imagined that the world of skilled labor, of trades and professions, might be accessible to someone like him.

"I... I think so," he said slowly. "I've always wondered how things work. How they're built, how they're fixed."

Rajan grunted, still focused on his work. "Most people don't wonder. They just want things to work and get angry when they don't." He paused, then added, "You can read?"

"A little," Arjun admitted. "I'm learning. Someone's been teaching me."

"Hm. Can you come back tomorrow? Same time?"

"Why?" Arjun asked, confused.

"Because I'm getting old and my back hurts from bending over these machines all day," Rajan said bluntly. "And because if you're actually interested and willing to learn, I could use an extra pair of hands occasionally. I won't pay you much—just a few rupees here and there—but I'll teach you. If you prove you're worth teaching."

Arjun's heart began to race. This was an opportunity—a real opportunity to learn something valuable, something that could lift him out of the endless cycle of scavenging.

"I'll come," he said immediately. "I'll work hard, sir. I promise."

Rajan finally looked at him fully, his weathered face unreadable. Then he nodded once. "We'll see. Now get out of here. You're blocking my light."

Arjun could barely contain his excitement when he told Meera about the encounter later that morning.

"He wants to teach you?" she asked, her eyes lighting up with genuine happiness. "Arjun, that's wonderful!"

"I don't know if it will amount to anything," he said, trying to temper his own hope. "He might decide I'm useless after a day or two. But even if I just learn a few things..."

"You'll learn everything," Meera said with conviction. "I know you will. You're quick and careful and you pay attention. Those are the things that matter."

Her faith in him was unwavering, and it both humbled and energized him. He wanted to prove her right, to become the person she seemed to see when she looked at him.

The next morning, Arjun arrived at Rajan's shop before dawn, his regular work already half-finished so he could dedicate time to learning. The old man was already there, brewing strong tea on a small kerosene stove.

"You're early," Rajan observed.

"I didn't want to be late, sir."

"Hm. Want tea?"

It was the first time in years that someone had offered to share their tea with him—not sold it, not grudgingly given it, but simply offered. Arjun nodded, too moved to speak.

They drank their tea in companionable silence, and then Rajan set him to work.

The tasks started simple: organizing tools, cleaning parts, holding things steady while Rajan worked. But Rajan talked as he worked, explaining what he was doing and why, pointing out the logic of machines, the principles of mechanics, the way different metals behaved under stress and heat.

Arjun absorbed it all like parched earth absorbing rain. He asked questions—tentatively at first, then more confidently as he realized Rajan didn't mind, even seemed to appreciate his curiosity.

"Why does this bolt strip so easily?"

"Because it's cheap steel. See the color? Soft. You need hardened steel for high-torque applications."

"How do you know which tool to use?"

"Experience mostly. But also understanding what you're trying to accomplish. You don't use a hammer when you need precision."

Day after day, Arjun returned. He worked for Rajan for an hour or two each morning, then continued his usual scavenging route to ensure he could still eat. It made his days longer, more exhausting, but he didn't care. Each day he learned something new—how to use a wrench properly, how to read technical diagrams, how to identify different types of metals by sight and feel, how to diagnose problems by sound and behavior.

Rajan was a strict teacher, quick to criticize mistakes but also quick to acknowledge improvement. "Better," he would grunt when Arjun did something correctly. "Not terrible," when Arjun showed promise. And once, after Arjun successfully diagnosed a faulty bearing on his own, "Good work."

Those two words felt like a benediction.

After a month of working with Rajan, Arjun received his first real payment—not the spare change he had expected, but a full fifty rupees.

"You've been useful," Rajan said gruffly, handing over the money. "You learn fast and you don't complain. Keep coming and I'll keep paying. Not much, but steady."

Fifty rupees for a month of morning work wasn't generous by any standard, but combined with his improved earnings from better-quality iron filings, it meant Arjun was now earning nearly double what he had been three months ago. More importantly, he was learning skills that could eventually lead to real employment—the kind of work that came with regular wages and didn't require crawling through garbage.

That evening, Arjun sat beneath his billboard and counted his savings. Two hundred and thirty rupees. It still wasn't much, but it felt like wealth. More than that, it felt like possibility.

The changes in Arjun weren't just financial. Meera noticed them too.

"You stand differently now," she observed one morning, tilting her head as she studied him. "More... confident."

Arjun hadn't noticed, but when he thought about it, he realized she was right. He no longer moved through the world with his shoulders hunched, his eyes downcast, trying to be invisible. He still worked hard, still got covered in dust and grime, but there was a purpose to it now beyond mere survival.

"Rajan says I have good hands," he told her, holding them up and examining them as though seeing them for the first time. They were still calloused, still stained with metal and oil, but now they were becoming skilled. "He says with more practice, I could be a decent mechanic."

"You could be more than decent," Meera said softly. "You could be excellent."

He smiled at her optimism, but secretly, he was beginning to believe it too.

One morning, Rajan surprised him with an offer.

"There's a factory opening a few streets over," the old man said, not looking up from the bearing he was cleaning. "They're looking for maintenance assistants. Basic work—cleaning machines, doing minor repairs, helping the senior mechanics. The pay is modest, but it's steady. Daily wages."

Arjun's heart leapt. "You think... you think I could do it?"

"I think you could try," Rajan said. "I know the factory supervisor. I could put in a word for you. But you'd need to present yourself properly—clean clothes, clean face, respectful attitude. They won't hire someone who looks like they crawled out of a garbage heap."

The words were harsh but true. Arjun looked down at himself—at the torn, filthy clothes that were the only ones he owned, at the permanent grime that seemed embedded in his skin no matter how hard he scrubbed.

"I don't have clean clothes," he admitted quietly.

Rajan sighed, reaching into a drawer and pulling out a folded shirt and a pair of trousers. They were old, worn, but clean and intact.

"These were my son's," he said gruffly. "He moved to the city years ago, doesn't need them anymore. They might be a bit big on you, but they'll do. Take them. Get yourself cleaned up—really cleaned up, not just a splash of water—and come see me tomorrow. I'll take you to meet the supervisor."

Arjun stared at the clothes, overwhelmed. "Sir, I can't—"

"You can and you will," Rajan interrupted. "Consider it an investment. If you get this job, you can pay me back by not embarrassing me in front of the supervisor."

That night, Arjun did something he hadn't done in months: he went to a public bathhouse that charged two rupees for a proper wash. He spent those two rupees without hesitation, scrubbing away layers of accumulated grime until his skin felt raw but clean. He washed his hair with cheap soap until it no longer felt stiff with dust. He used a broken piece of mirror to check his reflection and barely recognized himself.

Without the mask of dirt, his features were sharper, more defined. His dark eyes stood out against his clean skin. He looked younger than his eighteen years, but also more serious, more determined.

He carefully put on Rajan's son's clothes. The shirt was indeed too big, hanging loose on his thin frame, but it was whole and clean. The trousers had to be rolled at the ankles, but they gave him an air of respectability he had never possessed before.

For the first time in his life, Arjun looked like someone who might have a future.

The next morning, before going to meet Rajan, he stopped at the broken wall to see Meera. When she saw him, her eyes widened in shock.

"Arjun?" she whispered, as though she wasn't sure it was really him.

"It's me," he said, suddenly self-conscious. "Do I look strange?"

"No," she said, stepping closer, her eyes shining. "You look... you look wonderful. Like a completely different person."

"Rajan gave me these clothes," he explained. "He's taking me to meet a factory supervisor today. About a job. A real job."

Meera's hand flew to her mouth, and tears sprang to her eyes. "Arjun, that's... that's amazing! I'm so happy for you!"

"I haven't gotten it yet," he cautioned, though he couldn't keep the smile from his face. "They might not want me."

"They will," Meera said with absolute certainty. "How could they not?"

She reached up and adjusted his collar, smoothing the fabric with a tenderness that made his breath catch. Their faces were close, closer than they had ever been, and for a moment the world narrowed to just the two of them—to the warmth of her hand on his shoulder, to the hope shining in her eyes, to the possibility humming in the air between them.

"Thank you," he said quietly. "For believing in me. For teaching me to read. For making me want to be more than I was."

"You were always more," Meera whispered. "You just needed the chance to show it."

The interview with the factory supervisor was brief and businesslike. The man—a stern-faced individual named Mr. Kapoor—asked Arjun a few questions about his experience, tested his ability to identify tools and follow simple instructions, and observed his demeanor.

Rajan stood to the side, his presence a silent endorsement.

"You've never worked in a factory before?" Mr. Kapoor asked.

"No, sir. But I've been learning mechanical work with Rajan sir for the past month. And before that, I spent years working in the industrial lanes, so I understand how factories operate."

"Can you read instructions?"

"Yes, sir. I'm still learning, but I can read basic instructions and I'm improving every day."

Mr. Kapoor studied him for a long moment, then nodded. "We'll try you for a week. Trial period. Forty rupees per day. If you work well and cause no problems, we'll make it permanent. You start tomorrow at seven in the morning. Don't be late."

Forty rupees per day.

Arjun did the mathematics quickly in his head. Nearly three hundred rupees per week. Over a thousand per month. It was more money than he had ever imagined earning, more than he had made in three or four months of scavenging.

"Thank you, sir," he managed to say, trying to keep his voice steady despite the joy exploding in his chest. "I won't disappoint you."

When he told Meera the news the next morning, she actually cried—tears of happiness that she didn't bother to hide.

"A thousand rupees a month," she repeated, as though saying it aloud would make it more real. "Arjun, that's... that's a real income. That's a life."

"It's a start," he said, though he was grinning so widely his face hurt. "It's not much yet, but it's steady. And if I work hard, if I keep learning, maybe I can advance. Maybe I can become a senior mechanic eventually, earn even more."

"You will," Meera said, her voice full of conviction. "I know you will."

They stood together in their usual spot by the broken wall, the morning sun casting long shadows across the dusty lane. Arjun was dressed in his work clothes now—the same ones Rajan had given him, carefully washed and dried each evening. He no longer carried his magnet stick and burlap sack. That part of his life was over.

"Everything is changing," he said softly, almost to himself.

"For the better," Meera added, squeezing his hand gently.

He looked down at their joined hands—hers small and delicate, his rough but now clean—and felt a surge of emotion so intense it nearly overwhelmed him. He had done this. Through his own effort, his own determination, his own refusal to accept that he was destined to remain nothing forever, he had changed his life.

And he had done it for her as much as for himself.

"One day," he said, his voice low but fierce with promise, "I'm going to have enough to offer you a real home. Not just dreams, but something concrete. Something safe. Somewhere you never have to worry about anyone hurting you or making you feel small."

Meera's eyes glistened with tears again, but she smiled through them. "You've already given me so much, Arjun. You've given me hope. You've given me someone who sees me. That's worth more than any home."

"You deserve both," he insisted. "And I'm going to make sure you get both."

As Arjun walked toward the factory for his first official day of work, he felt lighter than he had in years. The weight of mere survival had been replaced by something different—the weight of responsibility, yes, but also the weight of purpose, of ambition, of love.

He was no longer just a scavenger, invisible and forgotten by the world.

He was Arjun—a young man with skills, with a job, with savings, and with someone worth becoming better for.

And for the first time in his eighteen years of life, he allowed himself to believe that the future might actually be kind to him.

The road ahead was still long and uncertain, filled with challenges he couldn't yet foresee. But he had taken the first real steps, and those steps had carried him further than he had ever dared to imagine.

From the dust of the industrial lanes, something new was rising.

And he was determined to see how high it could go.

When Worlds Collide

For two glorious weeks, Arjun's life felt almost charmed. He worked at the factory from seven in the morning until four in the afternoon, learning the rhythms of industrial machinery, proving himself reliable and quick to learn. His supervisor, Mr. Kapoor, had already commented favorably on his work ethic, and the other workers had begun to accept him as one of their own rather than just a trial employee.

Each morning before work, he still met Meera at their spot by the broken wall. The routine had changed—he no longer came covered in dust with a magnet stick, no longer left heavy sacks for her to guard—but the essence remained the same. They talked, they shared small moments of joy and hope, and they carefully nurtured the connection that had become the center of both their lives.

Arjun had even begun looking at small rental rooms in the cheaper parts of the city, calculating how many months of savings it would take before he could afford a place of his own. It was premature, perhaps even foolish, but he couldn't help himself. For the first time, he was planning a future that extended beyond the next meal, the next day.

But happiness, Arjun was about to learn, could be as fragile as it was precious.

It happened on a Tuesday morning, three weeks after Arjun had started his factory job.

He arrived at the broken wall a few minutes earlier than usual, eager to tell Meera about a small raise Mr. Kapoor had mentioned might be coming his way. The morning was cool and pleasant, and Arjun felt lighter than air as he walked the familiar route to their meeting place.

But when he turned the corner into the lane, his steps faltered.

Meera was there, but she wasn't alone.

A man stood beside her—middle-aged, with a stern face and the bearing of someone accustomed to authority. He wore simple but neat clothes, and his hand gripped Meera's arm tightly, possessively. Even from a distance, Arjun could see the tension in Meera's body, the fear in her eyes.

Uncle Ramesh.

It had to be.

Arjun's first instinct was to turn and leave, to avoid the confrontation that was clearly coming. But Meera had seen him, and the look in her eyes—pleading, apologetic, frightened—rooted him to the spot.

He walked forward slowly, his heart hammering in his chest.

"So," Uncle Ramesh said, his voice cold and hard, "this is him. This is the boy you've been sneaking out to meet every morning."

Meera's voice was barely a whisper. "Uncle, please—"

"Quiet," he snapped, and she flinched. His eyes fixed on Arjun with undisguised contempt. "What's your name, boy?"

Arjun lifted his chin, forcing himself to meet the man's gaze despite the fear churning in his stomach. "Arjun, sir."

"Arjun what? What's your family name? Where do you come from? What do your parents do?"

Each question was a hammer blow, designed to expose exactly what Arjun was: nobody, from nowhere, with nothing.

"I don't have a family name, sir," Arjun said, keeping his voice as steady as he could. "My father left when I was young. My mother died when I was born. I've been on my own for most of my life."

Uncle Ramesh's lip curled in disgust. "A street rat. I should have known." He turned to Meera, his grip on her arm tightening until she winced. "This is who you've been wasting your time with? This is who you've been lying for? A homeless beggar?"

"He's not a beggar," Meera said, her voice stronger now despite her fear. "He works. He has a job at a factory. He's—"

"I don't care if he's the factory owner," Uncle Ramesh interrupted harshly. "You have no business meeting with any boy, especially not one like this. Do you have any idea what people would say if they knew? Do you have any idea how this reflects on us, on our family?"

"We haven't done anything wrong," Meera protested. "We just talk. He's been kind to me. He's my friend."

"Friend," Uncle Ramesh spat the word like a curse. "Girls like you don't have friends like him. Girls like you—girls living under my roof, eating my food—have responsibilities. You have a debt to repay for the charity we've shown you."

The words hit Arjun like physical blows. Charity. That's how this man saw Meera's presence in his home—not as family, but as a burden he had magnanimously agreed to bear.

"Sir," Arjun said, his voice quiet but firm, "I respect that Meera lives under your care. But we haven't done anything dishonorable. We've only talked. She's been teaching me to read and write. That's all."

Uncle Ramesh's eyes narrowed dangerously. "You think I believe that? You think I'm a fool? I know what happens when girls sneak around with boys. I know what 'just talking' leads to."

"It's true, Uncle," Meera said desperately. "Please, you have to believe me. Arjun has never been anything but respectful. He's never—"

"Enough!" Uncle Ramesh's voice cracked like a whip. "I'm not interested in your excuses. This ends today. You will not come here again. You will not meet with this boy again. You will stay home where you belong and remember your place in our household."

He began to drag Meera away, and she looked back at Arjun with anguish in her eyes.

"Wait," Arjun said, stepping forward. "Please, sir. Don't punish her for my sake. If you're angry, be angry at me. But don't—"

"Don't tell me what to do with my own family," Uncle Ramesh snarled, turning on him. "You have no rights here, no voice. You're nothing. Less than nothing. A piece of trash that somehow learned to stand upright and pretend to be human."

The words were designed to cut, to diminish, to remind Arjun of exactly how worthless the world considered him. And they succeeded. Arjun felt himself shrinking under the verbal assault, felt the old familiar shame creeping back—the shame of being unwanted, unvalued, invisible.

But then he looked at Meera, saw the tears streaming down her face, saw the way she was looking at him with something that wasn't shame but desperate apology, and something hardened inside him.

"I may not have a family or a name or anything else the world values," Arjun said, his voice low but steady. "But I'm not nothing. I work honestly. I earn my keep. I don't hurt anyone. And I care about Meera more than anyone in your household seems to."

The moment the words left his mouth, he knew he had gone too far.

Uncle Ramesh's face darkened with rage. He released Meera's arm and took a step toward Arjun, his hand rising as though to strike.

"How dare you," he hissed. "How dare you speak to me that way. I should beat you bloody right here—"

"Uncle, no!" Meera threw herself between them, her arms outstretched protectively toward Arjun. "Please! Please don't hurt him!"

The desperation in her voice stopped Uncle Ramesh's hand mid-swing, but it also confirmed his worst suspicions. He stared at his niece, at the way she shielded this street boy with her own body, and something like realization and disgust crossed his face.

"You care for him," he said slowly, as though the words themselves were distasteful. "You actually care for this... this garbage picker."

"He's not—" Meera started, but Uncle Ramesh cut her off.

"I don't want to hear it. You're coming home. Now. And if I ever—ever—catch you near him again, you'll be out on the street. Do you understand me? I'll throw you out with nothing, and you can see how kind the world is to girls with no family and no protection."

The threat hung in the air, brutal and absolute. Meera's face went white, and Arjun saw her sway slightly, as though the weight of those words had physically struck her.

"Please," she whispered. "Uncle, please don't—"

"Come," Uncle Ramesh commanded, grabbing her arm again and pulling her away. "We're leaving. And you," he turned to fix Arjun with a final, vicious stare, "stay away from her. If I see you near her, near my house, near anyone in my family, I'll have you arrested. I know people. I can make your miserable life even more miserable. Do you understand?"

Arjun couldn't speak. He could only nod, his throat tight with helpless rage and grief.

Uncle Ramesh dragged Meera away, and she looked back once, her eyes locked with Arjun's, full of tears and unspoken apologies and something that looked heartbreakingly like goodbye.

Then they turned the corner and were gone.

Arjun stood alone in the empty lane for a long time after they left, his mind reeling, his heart feeling like it had been torn from his chest.

How had Uncle Ramesh found out? Had someone seen them and told him? Had Meera made a mistake, said something that gave them away? It didn't matter. The damage was done.

He thought about Uncle Ramesh's threat—to throw Meera out if she saw Arjun again. It wasn't an idle threat. Arjun had seen enough of the world to know that girls without family protection were vulnerable in ways he couldn't fully protect her from, not yet, not with his meager savings and uncertain employment.

If Meera was thrown out because of him, where would she go? What would happen to her? The thought was unbearable.

But so was the thought of never seeing her again, of losing the one person who had made his life feel worth living.

He went to work that day in a daze, going through the motions mechanically while his mind churned with useless questions and impossible scenarios. His coworkers noticed his distraction, but no one said anything. They had learned he was quiet, private, not one to share his troubles.

After work, instead of going back to his sleeping spot beneath the billboard, Arjun walked. He walked through the industrial lanes, past the broken wall where he had first seen Meera, through neighborhoods he had never explored before. He walked until his feet ached and the sun began to set, painting the polluted sky in shades of orange and purple.

Eventually, he found himself near the area where he knew Meera's uncle lived. He didn't know the exact house—Meera had never told him, perhaps sensing that knowing would be dangerous—but he knew the general neighborhood.

He stayed at a distance, watching people come and go, looking for any glimpse of her. It was foolish, reckless even. If Uncle Ramesh saw him here, he would make good on his threat. But Arjun couldn't help himself. He needed to know she was all right, needed some sign that she hadn't been hurt because of him.

But evening turned to night, and he saw nothing. Finally, knowing he was risking too much, he turned away and began the long walk back to his billboard.

The days that followed were among the darkest of Arjun's life.

He continued going to work, continued earning his wages, continued the routines he had built. But the joy had drained out of everything. The factory felt like a prison. The money he saved felt meaningless. The future he had been planning felt like a cruel joke.

What was the point of any of it without Meera?

Each morning, he woke with the instinctive urge to go to the broken wall, only to remember that she wouldn't be there. Some mornings, he went anyway, standing in the empty lane like a ghost haunting the scene of his own happiness, hoping against hope that she might somehow appear.

She never did.

After a week of this misery, Rajan noticed.

"You've been distracted," the old mechanic said one morning when Arjun came to help him before work. "Making sloppy mistakes. Your mind is somewhere else."

Arjun didn't deny it. "I'm sorry, sir."

Rajan studied him for a long moment. "Girl trouble?"

The perceptiveness surprised Arjun enough that he looked up. Rajan's weathered face showed understanding rather than judgment.

"Her family found out about us," Arjun said quietly. "They forbade her from seeing me. Threatened to throw her out if she disobeys."

"And you're thinking about doing something stupid," Rajan said. It wasn't a question.

"I don't know what to do," Arjun admitted, his voice cracking slightly. "I can't just forget about her. But if I try to see her, I'll only make things worse for her."

Rajan was silent for a moment, then sighed. "Let me tell you something, boy. When I was young, I was in love with a girl whose family thought I wasn't good enough. Her father was a merchant, relatively wealthy. I was a mechanic's apprentice, just like you are now. They refused to let us marry."

"What did you do?" Arjun asked.

"I worked," Rajan said simply. "I worked harder than I had ever worked in my life. I saved every rupee. I learned every skill I could. I made myself into someone her father couldn't dismiss so easily. It took three years, but eventually, I had my own shop, my own income, my own reputation. And when I went back to ask for her hand, her father couldn't say no."

"Did it work?" Arjun asked, though he was afraid of the answer.

Rajan smiled—a rare expression on his usually gruff face. "We were married for forty-two years before she passed. Had three children, five grandchildren. It was worth every moment of those three years I spent proving myself."

The story offered a glimmer of hope, but also a sobering reality. Three years. Could Arjun wait three years? Could Meera?

"I don't have three years," Arjun said. "I don't even know if she's all right. For all I know, they could be marrying her off to someone else right now, just to get rid of the problem."

Rajan's expression grew serious. "Then you need to find out. But carefully. Don't go charging in like a fool. That won't help anyone."

That evening, Arjun made a decision.

He would write her a letter.

It was risky—if it fell into the wrong hands, it could make everything worse. But he had to try. He had to let her know he hadn't abandoned her, that he was still thinking of her, that he was working toward a future where they could be together without fear.

Using the reading and writing skills Meera herself had taught him, Arjun carefully composed a letter on a scrap of paper he had taken from the factory. His handwriting was crude, the spelling uncertain in places, but the words came from his heart:

Meera,

I don't know if you will get this letter or if it will only bring you more trouble. But I had to try to reach you.

I am sorry for what happened. Sorry that knowing me has caused you pain. Your uncle was right about one thing—I am nobody. But I am trying to become somebody.

I have kept my job. I am saving money. I am learning. Every day I work, I think of you. Every rupee I save is for our future, if you still want one with me.

I know your uncle forbid you to see me. I know you have to obey him because you have no choice. I don't blame you. I understand.

But I want you to know I haven't forgotten you. I won't forget you. And when I am ready—when I have enough to offer you a real home, a real life—I will come back. I will ask for you properly. I will prove to your uncle and everyone else that I am worthy of you.

Please wait for me if you can. Please know that you gave me something no one else ever has—hope. And I won't waste it.

Yours,

Arjun

The next morning, before dawn, Arjun went to the neighborhood where Meera's uncle lived. He found a young boy playing in the street and paid him five rupees—a significant sum for a child—to deliver the letter to Meera specifically, in private if possible.

"There's a girl living in one of these houses," Arjun described her as best he could. "Her name is Meera. Can you find her and give her this?"

The boy, eager for the money, nodded enthusiastically and ran off.

Arjun watched him go, then walked away quickly, before he could be seen.

He didn't know if the letter would reach her. He didn't know if she would be able to respond. He didn't even know if she still wanted to hear from him after all the trouble he had caused.

But he had done what he could. He had reached out across the distance Uncle Ramesh had forced between them.

Now all he could do was work, save, and hope that somehow, someday, it would be enough.

Three days later, Arjun was leaving the factory after his shift when someone called his name.

"Arjun!"

He turned to see the same boy he had paid to deliver the letter, running toward him with something clutched in his hand.

"The girl—Meera—she asked me to give you this," the boy panted, thrusting a folded piece of paper into Arjun's hand. "She said to tell you: 'I'm waiting.'"

Before Arjun could respond or even thank him, the boy ran off, disappearing into the crowd.

With trembling hands, Arjun unfolded the paper. The handwriting was much neater than his, the spelling perfect, the words economical:

Arjun,

I received your letter. I cannot write much—Aunt watches me closely now.

I am all right. They have not hurt me, only restricted me. I told them you and I were only friends, that you were teaching me about the factories. They don't believe me, but they have no proof otherwise.

Uncle is looking for a marriage match for me. They want to arrange something quickly, to "settle the matter." I am scared.

But I am also waiting. I don't know how long I can wait, but I will try. Please be careful. Please keep working toward our future.

I think of you every morning at the time we used to meet.

Yours,
Meera

Arjun read the letter three times, his heart aching with every word. She was scared. Uncle Ramesh was trying to marry her off. Time was running out.

He folded the letter carefully and tucked it into his pocket, close to his heart.

Then he did the only thing he could do: he went back to his billboard, counted his savings—now four hundred rupees—and made a silent vow.

He would work harder. Save faster. Learn more. Prove himself worthy not in three years, but in months. Weeks, if possible.

Because Meera was waiting. And he would not let her wait in vain.

Calculated Risks

The words "Uncle is looking for a marriage match" haunted Arjun's every waking moment. They echoed in his mind while he worked at the factory, while he helped Rajan in the mornings, while he lay sleepless beneath the billboard at night, staring at the indifferent stars.

Four hundred rupees. That's all he had managed to save. It was more than he'd ever possessed in his life, but it was nowhere near enough. Nowhere near what he would need to rent a proper room, to establish himself as someone Uncle Ramesh couldn't dismiss, to offer Meera a life that wouldn't make her situation worse than it already was.

At his current rate—saving perhaps fifty or sixty rupees a week after eating and other necessities—it would take him months to accumulate enough. And he didn't have months. Every day that passed was another day Uncle Ramesh might find a suitable match for Meera, another day closer to losing her forever.

He needed more money, faster. But how?

The answer, when it came, arrived from an unexpected source.

It was late afternoon at the factory, and Arjun was helping to clean one of the large metal-cutting machines when he overheard a conversation between Mr. Kapoor and another supervisor.

"The night shift is still short three workers," the other supervisor was saying, his voice frustrated. "Ever since Mohan and the others left for that construction job, we've been struggling to meet the production quotas."

"I know," Mr. Kapoor replied, sounding equally stressed. "But finding reliable night workers isn't easy. Most people don't want to work those hours, and the ones who do are often unreliable."

"What about offering better pay? Double shift rates might attract some of the day workers."

"The manager approved it last week. Fifty rupees for a six-hour night shift, from ten at night until four in the morning. But so far, no one's taken it. The day workers say they're too tired, they have families, they need their sleep."

Fifty rupees for six hours. Arjun's mind began calculating immediately. If he worked his regular day shift from seven to four, he could rest for a few hours, then work the night shift from ten to four in the morning. That would be fifty plus forty—ninety rupees a day. Over six hundred rupees a week. More than double what he was currently making.

It would be exhausting. Brutal, even. He would be working nearly sixteen hours a day with only scattered hours of sleep. But it would also mean he could save money at more than twice his current rate. What would take months at his current pace could be accomplished in weeks.

The question was: could his body handle it?

He thought of Meera's letter, of the fear in her words. Uncle is looking for a marriage match. He thought of her waiting, hoping, trusting that he would find a way.

The answer was clear. He had to try.

After his shift ended, Arjun approached Mr. Kapoor directly.

"Sir, I heard you talking about needing night shift workers," he said, his heart pounding. "I'd like to take one of those positions."

Mr. Kapoor looked at him with surprise. "You? But you already work the day shift. That would be—" he paused, calculating, "—sixteen hours a day. That's not sustainable, Arjun. You'll burn yourself out within a week."

"I'm young and strong, sir. I can handle it. And I need the extra money."

Mr. Kapoor studied him for a long moment, his expression thoughtful. "Family troubles?"

Arjun hesitated, then nodded. It was close enough to the truth.

"Listen, boy," Mr. Kapoor said, his voice gentler than usual. "I appreciate your dedication, and God knows we need the workers. But I've seen men try to work double shifts before. It always ends badly—mistakes, accidents, exhaustion. I can't have you injuring yourself or others because you're too tired to think straight."

"Give me two weeks," Arjun said, hearing the desperation in his own voice but unable to contain it. "Let me prove I can do it. If my work quality drops, if I make mistakes, you can take me off the night shift. But please, sir. I need this."

Mr. Kapoor sighed, clearly torn between his need for workers and his concern for Arjun's wellbeing. Finally, he nodded.

"Two weeks. Trial basis. But the moment I see your performance slipping, you're done. Understood?"

"Yes, sir. Thank you, sir."

That night, Arjun reported for his first night shift at ten o'clock, having rested for only four hours. The factory at night was a different beast—darker, louder, with fewer workers and an atmosphere of isolation that felt almost oppressive. The machines roared and clanged, their sounds amplified by the emptiness.

His job on the night shift was similar to his day work—basic maintenance, cleaning, helping the machine operators with minor repairs and adjustments. The work itself wasn't harder, but doing it while fighting exhaustion was its own form of torture.

By two in the morning, Arjun's eyes were burning and his body ached with fatigue. By three, he was moving on autopilot, forcing himself to focus through sheer willpower. By four, when the shift finally ended, he stumbled out of the factory feeling like he had aged ten years in six hours.

He had just enough time to return to his billboard, collapse into sleep for two and a half hours, then drag himself up to begin his day shift at seven.

The second day was worse. The third day, worse still.

By the end of the first week, Arjun felt like a walking corpse. His hands shook constantly from exhaustion. His eyes were sunken and bloodshot. His body moved through the motions of work, but his mind felt foggy, distant, barely tethered to consciousness.

But he didn't quit. And more importantly, he didn't make mistakes. He worked with an almost manic focus, knowing that any error could cost him this opportunity.

Mr. Kapoor watched him carefully throughout that first week, his expression a mixture of concern and grudging respect. On the seventh day, he pulled Arjun aside.

"I don't know how you're doing this," the supervisor said, shaking his head. "But your work hasn't suffered. If anything, you've been more careful than before. Are you sure you want to continue?"

"Yes, sir," Arjun said, his voice hoarse from exhaustion. "I'm sure."

"All right. The trial period is over. The position is yours for as long as you want it. But please, boy—take care of yourself. Money isn't worth dying for."

But Arjun knew it wasn't about the money, not really. It was about what the money represented: hope, possibility, a future with Meera. And that was worth any amount of exhaustion.

As the days turned into weeks, Arjun fell into a grueling but effective routine. He slept in fragments—two hours here, three hours there—snatching rest whenever he could. He ate cheaply but sufficiently, knowing he needed fuel to sustain the brutal schedule. Every other expense was eliminated, every rupee saved with obsessive discipline.

His savings grew with remarkable speed: four hundred became six hundred, six hundred became eight hundred, eight hundred became a thousand.

But the physical toll was undeniable. He grew thinner, his already lean frame becoming almost skeletal. Dark circles permanently settled beneath his eyes. His hands developed a tremor that never quite went away. Other workers began to comment on his appearance, asking if he was sick, if he needed help.

"I'm fine," he would say, waving off their concerns. "Just working hard."

Rajan was less easily dismissed. The old mechanic took one look at Arjun during one of their morning sessions and grabbed him by the shoulder.

"You're killing yourself," Rajan said bluntly. "Whatever you're doing, it's not worth your health."

"It's worth it," Arjun insisted. "I'm making good money. Saving fast."

"For what? What good is money if you're dead?"

"I'm not going to die," Arjun said, though he wondered sometimes if that was true. "I just need to do this for a little while longer. Until I have enough."

"Enough for what?"

Arjun hesitated, then told him—about Meera, about her uncle's threat to arrange her marriage, about his desperate need to prove himself worthy before it was too late.

Rajan listened in silence, his weathered face grave. When Arjun finished, the old man sighed deeply.

"I understand now," he said. "But listen to me, boy. What you're doing—it's noble, but it's also foolish. You can't help her if you work yourself into an early grave. You need to be smarter about this."

"I don't have time to be smart," Arjun said desperately. "I need money, as much as I can get, as fast as I can get it."

Rajan was quiet for a moment, thinking. Then he said, "There might be another way. A faster way. But it's risky."

Arjun's attention sharpened immediately. "What do you mean?"

"You know the scrap market, don't you? Not the small junkyards where you used to sell iron filings, but the big wholesale markets where factories sell bulk metal waste?"

"I've heard of them," Arjun said. "But I've never been there. Those are for big operators with trucks and capital."

"True," Rajan agreed. "But there's an opportunity there if you're smart and brave. The factories sell their scrap at fixed rates to wholesalers, who then process it and sell it to smelters for much higher prices. The profit margin is significant—sometimes double or triple the purchase price."

"I don't have enough money to buy factory scrap in bulk," Arjun said, confused about where this was going.

"No, but you might have enough to buy smaller lots at the wholesale market," Rajan explained. "Sometimes individual sellers come there—small workshops, mechanics like me, people who've accumulated metal waste but don't have direct connections to smelters. They sell to middlemen who mark up the prices. If you could buy from these small sellers and sell directly to smelters, you could make good profit."

"How much profit are we talking about?" Arjun asked.

"It depends on your negotiation skills and luck. But potentially? You could double your money in a few days. Maybe more if you're smart about what you buy."

The possibility was tantalizing. If Arjun took his thousand rupees of savings, invested it in scrap metal, and doubled it, he'd have two thousand. Do it again, and he'd have four thousand—more than enough to prove to Uncle Ramesh that he was a man of substance, someone worthy of consideration.

But there was a catch. There was always a catch.

"What's the risk?" Arjun asked.

Rajan's expression grew serious. "Several. First, you could buy bad metal—contaminated, wrong type, something that smelters won't pay premium for. Second, you could get cheated—sellers lying about weight or quality. Third, prices fluctuate. What's valuable one week might be less valuable the next. And fourth—this is the big one—if you invest all your savings and it goes wrong, you lose everything. All that work, all that exhaustion, all those double shifts—gone."

The risks were substantial. Arjun thought about his thousand rupees, earned through weeks of sixteen-hour days, through exhaustion and sacrifice. Losing it all would be devastating, would set him back to zero.

But he also thought about Meera, waiting, hoping, fighting against an arranged marriage she didn't want. He thought about time running out, about the need to act before it was too late.

"How do I learn?" he asked. "How do I know what to buy, where to sell?"

A slight smile crossed Rajan's face. "You ask someone who's been doing this for forty years. I know the market, boy. I know the sellers, the smelters, the good deals from the bad. If you want, I can take you there. Teach you what to look for. But the decision to invest—that has to be yours."

That night, after his shift, Arjun sat beneath his billboard with his savings pouch in his hands. One thousand, one hundred and thirty rupees. Every coin represented hours of his life, sweat, exhaustion, sacrifice.

He could play it safe—continue working double shifts, continue saving slowly but surely. In another month or two, he might have enough to approach Uncle Ramesh with a proposal.

Or he could take the risk—invest his savings in the scrap market, potentially doubling or tripling his money in a fraction of the time.

He thought about Meera's letter. Uncle is looking for a marriage match. I am scared.

Time was not his friend. Safety was a luxury he couldn't afford.

He made his decision.

The next day was his day off—a rare occurrence in his current schedule—and he asked Rajan to take him to the wholesale scrap market.

The market was located on the outskirts of the city, a vast open area filled with mountains of metal in various forms—sheets, pipes, wires, machinery parts, unidentifiable chunks that had once been something but were now just raw material waiting for rebirth.

Trucks rumbled in and out constantly. Men shouted prices, argued, negotiated. The air smelled of rust and oil and possibility.

Rajan guided him through the chaos, pointing out different sections, explaining the economics.

"Copper is always valuable—highest price per kilo. But it's expensive to buy and often contaminated with other metals. Brass is good too, but harder to find. Steel is cheap but heavy—you can make money on volume. Aluminum is light and valuable, but you need to know your grades."

They spent hours walking through the market, with Rajan introducing Arjun to various sellers and smelter representatives, establishing connections, building the network Arjun would need to operate here.

Finally, near the end of the day, Rajan stopped at a small section where an elderly man was selling what looked like copper wire—thick industrial cables that had been stripped from old buildings.

"How much?" Rajan asked, examining the wire carefully.

"Eighteen rupees per kilo," the seller said. "Good quality copper, minimal contamination."

Rajan inspected the wire more closely, then nodded. "It's fair. Smelters are paying thirty-two rupees per kilo for this grade right now. If you buy at eighteen and sell at thirty-two, minus transport costs, you're looking at about twelve rupees profit per kilo."

He turned to Arjun. "How much capital do you want to risk?"

Arjun's hands trembled slightly as he calculated. "I have eleven hundred rupees. If I keep a hundred for safety... that's a thousand rupees. At eighteen per kilo, that's about fifty-five kilos of copper."

"And if you sell it at thirty-two per kilo, minus transport and handling, you'll walk away with about sixteen hundred to seventeen hundred rupees," Rajan confirmed. "A clean profit of six to seven hundred rupees for a few days of work."

It was more than Arjun made in two weeks of double shifts. The temptation was overwhelming.

But so was the fear. What if the smelter didn't pay the expected price? What if the copper was contaminated and worth less than they thought? What if he got cheated somewhere in the process?

"What do you think?" Arjun asked Rajan. "Should I do it?"

The old mechanic looked at him seriously. "I can't make this decision for you, boy. But I'll tell you this—I've known this seller for twenty years. He's honest. The copper looks good. The market price is stable right now. If you're going to take a risk, this is a relatively safe one."

Arjun took a deep breath. He thought of Meera one more time, of her waiting, of the unknown suitor her uncle might be negotiating with at this very moment.

"I'll do it," he said.

The transaction was completed quickly. Arjun handed over one thousand rupees—nearly everything he had saved—and in return received about fifty-five kilograms of copper wire bundled in manageable loads. Rajan arranged for a small cart to transport it to a smelter he trusted, and they delivered it the next morning.

The smelter examined the copper carefully, testing its purity, weighing it precisely. Then he made his offer: "Thirty rupees per kilo. Final price."

It was slightly less than Rajan had hoped, but still profitable. Arjun did the math quickly: fifty-five kilos at thirty rupees each was sixteen hundred and fifty rupees. Minus the transport costs and a small fee to the cart operator, he was left with about fifteen hundred and eighty rupees.

He had invested one thousand and walked away with fifteen hundred and eighty.

Five hundred and eighty rupees profit in three days.

The relief was so intense that Arjun's knees nearly buckled. He had taken the risk, and it had paid off. Not spectacularly, not enough to solve all his problems, but enough to prove that the strategy could work.

"Well done," Rajan said, genuine pride in his voice. "You just completed your first real business transaction. How does it feel?"

"Terrifying," Arjun admitted. "But also... empowering."

"That's what risk is," Rajan said. "Terrifying and empowering in equal measure. The question is—will you do it again?"

Arjun looked at the money in his hands. Fifteen hundred and eighty rupees. If he did this again and again, carefully, intelligently, he could reach his goal far faster than he ever imagined.

"Yes," he said. "I'll do it again."

Over the following weeks, Arjun developed a pattern. He continued working his double shifts at the factory—he needed the steady income to live on and to have capital for his scrap transactions. But every few days, on his rare breaks, he would go to the market with Rajan, look for opportunities, invest, and sell.

Not every transaction was as profitable as the first. One time he lost money on a batch of steel that turned out to be lower quality than advertised. Another time he broke even, barely covering his costs. But more often than not, he made money—sometimes a hundred rupees, sometimes three hundred, once nearly five hundred.

His savings grew exponentially: fifteen hundred became two thousand, two thousand became three thousand.

But the pace was taking its toll. He was now working sixteen-hour days at the factory while also managing his side business in the scrap market. He slept perhaps three or four hours a night. He ate irregularly, often forgetting meals in his rush between obligations. His body was running on pure adrenaline and determination.

Other workers began to notice his deteriorating condition. Mr. Kapoor pulled him aside one day, his expression concerned.

"Arjun, I don't know what you're doing in your off hours, but you look terrible. You're losing weight, you have constant tremors, and yesterday I saw you nearly fall asleep standing up. This can't continue."

"I'm fine, sir," Arjun lied. "Just a little tired."

"A little tired? Boy, you look like death. I'm serious—if you don't take care of yourself, I'm going to have to remove you from the night shift. I can't risk you having an accident."

The threat was real, and Arjun knew it. He also knew that Mr. Kapoor was right—he was pushing his body beyond reasonable limits. But he was so close now. Three thousand rupees. Maybe another few weeks, another few good transactions, and he'd have enough to approach Uncle Ramesh with a real proposal.

"I understand, sir," Arjun said. "I'll be more careful."

But being careful wasn't really an option. Not when time was running out.

One evening, after a particularly long day, Arjun received another message through the street boy who had become his unofficial courier. This time, Meera's note was even shorter than before:

A.

Uncle has found someone. A man from another city, a clerk with a steady job. They are discussing terms. The wedding might be in two months.

Please hurry.

M.

Two months.

Arjun stared at the note, his hands shaking—though whether from exhaustion or panic, he couldn't tell.

Two months wasn't enough time to save the safe way. But it might be enough if he took bigger risks, made bolder moves.

He counted his savings again. Three thousand, two hundred rupees. He was getting close, but he wasn't there yet. Uncle Ramesh wouldn't be impressed by three thousand rupees. He needed more—enough to prove he could provide for Meera, enough to offer security and stability.

He needed at least five thousand. Maybe six to be safe.

Which meant he needed to risk everything one more time. Take his entire three thousand, invest it in a single transaction, and hope for a big return.

It was foolish. It was dangerous. If anything went wrong, he'd lose everything he'd worked for.

But if he didn't try, he'd lose Meera anyway.

The choice, once again, was no choice at all.

The next day, Arjun went to Rajan with a proposal.

"I need to make one big transaction," he told the old mechanic. "I need to invest everything—all three thousand rupees—and turn it into five or six thousand. What's the best way to do that?"

Rajan's expression darkened. "That's a dangerous game, boy. Investing everything in a single transaction? One mistake and you're ruined."

"I know the risks," Arjun said. "But I don't have time for small, safe moves anymore. Meera's uncle is arranging her marriage. I have maybe two months. I need to make something happen now."

Rajan studied him for a long moment, then sighed heavily. "There is one option. It's risky, but if it works, you could potentially double your money. Maybe more."

"Tell me," Arjun said.

And Rajan began to explain his plan—one that would require everything Arjun had learned, all his courage, and a significant amount of luck.

It was risky, perhaps even reckless.

But it was also his only chance.

And Arjun, who had started life with nothing and had clawed his way to this precarious moment of possibility, was willing to risk everything for the one person who had made his life worth living.

"I'll do it," he said.

CHAPTER TEN

The Reckoning

Rajan's plan was audacious in its simplicity and terrifying in its stakes.

A large construction company was demolishing an old factory building on the edge of the city. The structure was being torn down to make way for a new commercial complex, and all the metal from the building—steel beams, copper wiring, aluminum fixtures, brass fittings—was being sold as scrap to clear the site quickly.

"The company wants to move fast," Rajan explained. "They're selling everything in one lot—all the metal from the building together. They haven't sorted it, haven't separated the valuable from the worthless. It's a bulk deal, sold by weight, one price for everything."

"How much are they asking?" Arjun had asked, his heart already racing.

"Four thousand rupees for approximately five hundred kilos of mixed metal. They want it gone by the end of the week."

Arjun had felt his stomach drop. "But I only have three thousand."

"I know," Rajan had said. "Which is why I'm offering to loan you the other thousand. With one condition—you pay me back twelve hundred. That's two hundred rupees interest."

It was a fair rate, actually generous given the risk Rajan was taking. But it also meant Arjun would be investing money he didn't have, banking on a return that wasn't guaranteed.

"What if the metal isn't as valuable as we think?" Arjun had asked.

"Then we both lose money," Rajan had said bluntly. "I'm risking my capital too. But I've seen the building. I've walked through it. There's good copper wiring throughout, solid steel beams, brass fixtures in the old offices. If we buy smart and sell to the right smelters, we could turn four thousand into eight or nine thousand. Maybe more."

Eight thousand rupees. It would be more than enough. More than Uncle Ramesh could dismiss. Enough to offer Meera not just promises but concrete proof of stability.

But if it failed, Arjun would lose everything and owe Rajan money he couldn't pay.

He had taken the deal.

The transaction had been completed three days ago. Arjun and Rajan, along with two hired laborers, had spent an entire day dismantling and hauling the metal from the demolished building. It was backbreaking work—cutting, sorting, loading, transporting. By the end of it, Arjun's hands were bleeding, his back screamed with pain, and every muscle in his body felt like it was on fire.

But they had done it. Five hundred kilos of mixed metal, now sorted into categories: copper, brass, aluminum, steel, and various alloys.

The sorting had taken another day. Rajan's experienced eye had been crucial—he could identify metal types at a glance, could estimate purity and grade with remarkable accuracy. They separated the valuable from the less valuable, cleaned what could be cleaned, and prepared everything for sale.

And then had come the nail-biting process of finding buyers.

The copper had gone to a smelter on the north side of the city—sixty-eight kilos at thirty-two rupees per kilo. Two thousand, one hundred and seventy-six rupees.

The brass had sold to a different buyer—forty-two kilos at twenty-six rupees per kilo. One thousand and ninety-two rupees.

The aluminum had been harder to move, but they'd finally found a buyer willing to pay twenty-two rupees per kilo for the forty kilos they had. Eight hundred and eighty rupees.

The steel and other metals had gone to a bulk buyer for a lower rate, but the sheer volume had added another thousand rupees.

In total, after all sales were complete and the laborers paid, they had netted five thousand, two hundred rupees.

After repaying Rajan his one thousand plus two hundred rupees interest, Arjun was left with exactly four thousand rupees.

Combined with the two hundred he had kept in reserve, his total savings stood at four thousand, two hundred rupees.

It wasn't the eight or nine thousand Rajan had optimistically projected. But it was enough. It had to be enough.

Arjun spent the next two days preparing for what would be the most important conversation of his life.

He went to a public bathhouse and paid for a thorough wash. He scrubbed every inch of his body until his skin was raw and clean, washed his hair until it shone, and even paid extra for a shave from the bathhouse barber.

He took his best clothes—the ones Rajan had given him months ago, now carefully maintained and clean—and had them pressed at a small ironing shop. He bought new sandals to replace the broken ones he'd been wearing. He even purchased a small bottle of cheap cologne, which he applied sparingly.

When he looked at himself in a shop window, he barely recognized the person staring back. He looked respectable. Presentable. Like someone who worked honestly and had prospects.

It would have to do.

On the morning he had decided to approach Uncle Ramesh, Arjun woke before dawn with his stomach in knots. He had barely slept the night before, running through speeches in his head, imagining every possible outcome of the conversation to come.

He dressed carefully, checked and rechecked that his savings were secure in a small cloth envelope tucked inside his shirt. Four thousand, two hundred rupees. His entire worth, his entire effort of the last months, compressed into paper and coins.

Before going to Uncle Ramesh's house, he stopped at a small temple near the industrial lanes. He wasn't particularly religious—life had never given him much reason to believe in divine benevolence—but in that moment, he felt the need for something beyond himself.

He stood before the temple's deity, hands folded, and whispered a prayer he'd heard others say but had never spoken himself: "Please. If there's any justice in this world, any kindness, let this work. Let me have earned the right to be with her."

The deity, stone and silent, offered no response. But Arjun felt fractionally steadier as he left.

Uncle Ramesh's house was modest but well-maintained—a small two-story structure with faded yellow paint and a narrow courtyard in front. It was mid-morning when Arjun arrived, and he could see a woman—presumably Aunt Lakshmi—hanging laundry on a line in the courtyard.

He stood at the gate for a long moment, gathering his courage. Every instinct screamed at him to run, to avoid the confrontation, to protect himself from the rejection that seemed inevitable.

But he thought of Meera—of her waiting, of her fear, of the arranged marriage looming over her like a sentence—and he pushed the gate open.

The sound of the gate's hinges drew Aunt Lakshmi's attention. She turned, squinting at him suspiciously. "What do you want?"

"Good morning, madam," Arjun said, keeping his voice respectful. "My name is Arjun. I've come to speak with Mr. Ramesh, if he's available."

Recognition dawned in her eyes, quickly followed by hostility. "You. You're that boy. The one who was meeting Meera."

"Yes, madam."

"You have some nerve coming here," she spat. "After my husband explicitly told you to stay away. Do you want to get yourself beaten? Or arrested?"

"I mean no disrespect," Arjun said, standing his ground despite his racing heart. "But I need to speak with Mr. Ramesh. It's important. It's about Meera."

"There's nothing to discuss," Aunt Lakshmi said coldly. "Meera's marriage is being arranged with a respectable man. She has no future with someone like you."

"Please," Arjun said, hearing the desperation in his own voice. "Just five minutes. That's all I ask. If Mr. Ramesh hears what I have to say and still wants me to leave, I will. I won't cause trouble. But please, let me speak with him."

Aunt Lakshmi looked like she wanted to refuse, but something in Arjun's demeanor—the cleanliness of his clothes, the steadiness of his voice, or perhaps simply the sheer audacity of his presence—made her hesitate.

"Wait here," she finally said, her tone making it clear she expected nothing good to come of this. "I'll see if he'll speak with you. But if he says no, you leave immediately. Understood?"

"Yes, madam. Thank you."

She disappeared into the house, and Arjun was left standing in the courtyard, his hands trembling despite his attempts to appear calm.

Several long minutes passed. Then Uncle Ramesh appeared in the doorway.

He looked much as Arjun remembered—stern-faced, solid, with the bearing of a man accustomed to being obeyed. His eyes fell on Arjun with a mixture of surprise and anger.

"You," he said, his voice low and dangerous. "I told you to stay away from my family. I should have you thrown out right now."

"Please, sir," Arjun said quickly. "I know you told me to stay away, and I have respected that. I haven't tried to contact Meera since that day. But I'm asking you—begging you—to give me just five minutes to speak with you. After that, if you want me gone, I'll leave and never bother you again."

Uncle Ramesh studied him, his expression hard. "What could you possibly have to say that would interest me?"

"I want to ask for permission to marry Meera," Arjun said, the words tumbling out before he could lose his nerve.

For a moment, Uncle Ramesh simply stared at him. Then he laughed—a harsh, incredulous sound devoid of humor.

"You? Marry Meera? You're even more delusional than I thought. You're a street rat. You have nothing. You are nothing. Why would I ever give my niece to someone like you?"

"Because I'm not nothing anymore," Arjun said, forcing his voice to remain steady. "I know what I was when you saw me last—a scavenger living on the streets, barely surviving. But I've changed, sir. I've worked, I've learned, I've built something."

"Built something?" Uncle Ramesh's tone was mocking. "What could you possibly have built in a few months?"

Arjun reached into his shirt and pulled out the cloth envelope. "I have a steady job at a factory. I work as a maintenance assistant, earning forty rupees a day. That's over twelve hundred rupees a month. I also have savings—four thousand, two hundred rupees."

He held out the envelope, and Uncle Ramesh's expression shifted from mockery to surprise. He took the envelope, opened it, and examined the contents with obvious disbelief.

"This is real money," Uncle Ramesh said slowly, as though he couldn't quite believe it. "Where did you get this? Did you steal it?"

"No, sir," Arjun said firmly. "I earned every rupee honestly. Through my factory work, through side business in the scrap metal trade, through saving every coin I could.

I can show you pay stubs from the factory if you don't believe me. I can introduce you to my supervisor, to my mentor who taught me the business. It's all legitimate."

Uncle Ramesh fell silent, examining Arjun with new eyes. The contempt hadn't entirely left his expression, but it had been joined by something else—uncertainty, perhaps, or the beginning of grudging respect.

"Even if this is true," Uncle Ramesh said finally, "four thousand rupees and a factory job doesn't make you suitable for Meera. She needs security, stability, a husband from a good family with proper background."

"With respect, sir, she needs someone who will value her, who will treat her with kindness, who will work hard to provide for her," Arjun said, his voice gaining strength. "I can't offer her a prestigious family name. I can't offer her social connections or a wealthy background. But I can offer her honesty, dedication, and a future we'll build together."

"You're asking me to entrust my niece to a man who was collecting garbage from streets just months ago," Uncle Ramesh said bluntly.

"Yes, sir, I am," Arjun said. "Because that man was hungry and desperate but still worked honestly. That man had nothing but refused to steal or beg. That man met your niece and found a reason to become more than he was. And he did become more—through his own effort, his own determination."

Arjun paused, then added quietly, "You said I was nothing. And maybe by your standards, I was. But I proved that nothing could become something. That's more than many men with fine family names ever accomplish."

The words hung in the air between them. Uncle Ramesh's expression was unreadable, but Arjun could see him thinking, processing, weighing.

"I've already found a match for Meera," Uncle Ramesh said finally. "A clerk from Pune. He has a stable government job, comes from a decent family. The discussions are well advanced."

"Then ask her what she wants," Arjun said. "Ask her if she wants to marry a stranger chosen for convenience, or if she wants to choose her own future."

"Girls don't always know what's best for them," Uncle Ramesh said, but there was less conviction in his voice now.

"Girls don't, or men don't want to give them the choice?" Arjun countered, more boldly than he'd intended.

Uncle Ramesh's eyes flashed with anger, and for a moment Arjun thought he'd pushed too far. But then the older man sighed, suddenly looking tired.

"Even if—and this is a very large 'if'—I were to consider your proposal, four thousand rupees isn't enough for a marriage. There would be expenses, arrangements, expectations."

"I know, sir," Arjun said. "Which is why I'm not asking to marry her tomorrow. I'm asking for permission to work toward marriage. Give me six months—just six months. Let me continue working, continue saving, continue proving myself. If at the end of that time you still don't think I'm worthy, then make whatever arrangement you think is best. But give me a chance to prove what I can become."

"And in those six months, you expect me to let you see Meera? Court her openly?"

"I'm asking for the chance to build a future worthy of her," Arjun said. "If that means seeing her under supervision, with your family present, I'll accept that. If it means not seeing her at all while I work, I'll accept that too. All I'm asking is that you don't finalize her marriage to someone else until I've had a chance to prove myself."

Uncle Ramesh was quiet for a long time, his gaze shifting between Arjun and the envelope of money still in his hands. Finally, he spoke.

"You have courage, I'll give you that. Stupidity too, but courage. Most men in your position wouldn't dare approach me like this."

"Most men in my position have something to lose," Arjun said. "I don't. Without Meera, nothing else matters anyway."

Another long silence. Then Uncle Ramesh made a decision.

"Six months," he said. "I'll give you six months to prove yourself. But there are conditions. You will not see Meera during this time. You will focus entirely on your work, on building your savings, on establishing yourself. At the end of six months, you will return here, and we will assess your situation properly. If you've made real progress—if you have stable employment, significant savings, and prospects for the future—I will consider allowing a formal courtship. Supervised, respectable, proper."

Arjun's heart soared. It wasn't a yes to marriage, but it was a chance. A real chance.

"And the other proposal?" he asked. "The clerk from Pune?"

"I'll tell them we need more time to consider," Uncle Ramesh said. "I'll delay. But Arjun—if you fail, if you waste this opportunity, I will finalize Meera's marriage to someone else. This is the only chance I'm giving you. Don't squander it."

"I won't, sir," Arjun said, his voice thick with emotion. "Thank you. Thank you for giving me this opportunity."

"Don't thank me yet," Uncle Ramesh said grimly. "Six months is a long time. A lot can go wrong. And even if you succeed financially, there's no guarantee I'll approve the marriage. You're still from nowhere, with no family, no background. But..." he paused, looking at Arjun with something that might have been the faintest hint of respect, "you've surprised me once already. Perhaps you'll surprise me again."

As Arjun left the house, his legs felt weak with relief and his hands still trembled. He had done it. He had faced Uncle Ramesh and emerged with a chance—slim, conditional, but real.

Six months. He had six months to turn his fragile progress into something undeniable.

It would be difficult. He would need to continue working brutally hard, continue taking calculated risks, continue sacrificing every comfort and convenience.

But he had done harder things. He had risen from nothing once already. He could do it again.

As he walked back through the streets toward his workplace, Arjun felt lighter than he had in weeks. The weight of uncertainty had been replaced by the weight of purpose. He knew what he needed to do. He knew the timeline. He knew the stakes.

Before he turned the corner that would take him out of sight of Uncle Ramesh's house, he glanced back one more time. And there, in a second-floor window, he saw her.

Meera.

She was watching him, her hand pressed against the glass. Even from this distance, he could see the question in her posture: What happened?

Arjun smiled—a genuine, hopeful smile—and raised his hand in a small wave.

The gesture said everything: Wait for me. I'm coming back. We have a chance.

Meera's hand moved to her heart, and even though Arjun couldn't see her face clearly, he knew she was crying. But he hoped—believed—they were tears of relief and hope rather than despair.

He turned away and continued walking, his mind already racing with plans.

Six months. One hundred and eighty days to transform his life completely.

It seemed impossible.

But then again, so had everything else he had accomplished since the day Meera first watched him from behind a broken wall.

And if there was one thing Arjun had learned, it was this: impossible was just another word for "not yet."

He was going to make Uncle Ramesh see what Meera already knew—that he was worthy. Not because of where he came from or what family name he carried, but because of what he had built with his own hands, his own mind, his own unbreakable determination.

The metal scavenger was becoming something more.

And in six months, he would return to claim his future.

Six Months Later

The six months had been the longest and shortest of Arjun's life—endless in their daily grind, yet somehow racing past with terrifying speed toward the deadline that would determine his entire future.

He had kept his promise to Uncle Ramesh. He had not tried to see Meera, had not sent messages, had not lingered near her uncle's house hoping for a glimpse of her. The discipline had been agonizing, but Arjun understood that this was part of the test—proving he could honor his word, that he could sacrifice immediate desire for long-term commitment.

But he had thought about her every day. Every morning when he woke before dawn. Every night when he finally collapsed into sleep. Every moment of grinding work and sacrifice, her face had been there in his mind, the reason behind every decision, every hardship endured.

And he had not wasted the opportunity Uncle Ramesh had given him.

In the first month, Arjun had continued his brutal double-shift schedule at the factory while carefully managing his scrap metal business. His reputation in both worlds had grown steadily. Mr. Kapoor had promoted him to senior maintenance assistant, which came with a raise to fifty-five rupees per day. It wasn't a fortune, but it was progress—tangible, documentable progress.

In the second month, Rajan had offered him a partnership of sorts. "You have good instincts for this business," the old mechanic had said. "And I'm getting too old to handle everything alone. What if we formalize our arrangement? You invest your capital, I provide my expertise and connections, we split the profits sixty-forty. You get the sixty—you're doing most of the physical work."

Arjun had accepted immediately. The partnership had allowed him to scale up his operations, to take on larger transactions with less personal risk. Rajan's network of buyers and sellers, combined with Arjun's willingness to work harder than anyone else, had proven remarkably profitable.

By the third month, Arjun had saved enough to finally leave the billboard. He had rented a small room—barely more than a closet, really, with just enough space for a thin mattress, a small shelf, and his belongings—but it was his. He had a door that locked. A roof that didn't leak. An address. For the first time in his life, when someone asked where he lived, he could give them an answer that wasn't "nowhere."

The fourth month had brought unexpected opportunity. One of the factory supervisors had mentioned that he was looking to sell his old motorcycle—a battered but functional vehicle that he no longer needed. The asking price was steep: three thousand rupees. But Arjun had recognized the value immediately. With a motorcycle, he could transport scrap metal himself, could reach more buyers and sellers, could eliminate the costs of hiring carts and laborers.

He had negotiated the price down to twenty-five hundred, bought the motorcycle, and spent the next few weeks teaching himself to ride it. The first week had been terrifying—he'd fallen twice, scraped his knees and palms, nearly crashed into a vendor's cart. But gradually, awkwardly, he had learned. And once he mastered it, his business efficiency had nearly doubled.

By the fifth month, Arjun's combined income from the factory, his partnership with Rajan, and his own scrap transactions was averaging nearly four hundred rupees per week. He was saving aggressively, spending only on absolute necessities. His room remained sparse, his meals simple, his clothes few but clean.

The numbers in his savings had climbed with steady determination: six thousand became eight thousand, eight thousand became ten thousand, ten thousand became twelve.

And now, as he stood outside Uncle Ramesh's house on the exact day that marked six months since their last conversation, Arjun possessed assets that would have seemed impossible to the boy who had once scraped iron filings from factory lanes:

Fourteen thousand, eight hundred rupees in savings

A steady factory job paying nearly seventeen hundred rupees per month

A profitable partnership in a scrap metal business averaging two thousand rupees per month in his share of profits

A functional motorcycle (worth approximately two thousand rupees)

A rented room with three months' advance rent already paid

Pay stubs, partnership documents, and character references from Mr. Kapoor and Rajan

He had transformed himself from a homeless scavenger into a man with prospects, with assets, with a future.

The question now was: would it be enough?

Arjun had dressed in new clothes for this meeting—not expensive, but new and well-fitted. He had visited a barber the previous evening, gotten a proper haircut and shave. He looked, he hoped, like a man who had his life together. Like someone who could provide for a wife.

He took a deep breath and knocked on Uncle Ramesh's gate.

Aunt Lakshmi answered, and her expression was complicated when she saw him—surprise, certainly, but also something that might have been grudging acknowledgment. He looked different than he had six months ago. More solid. More real.

"He's expecting you," she said simply, without the hostility of their previous encounter. "Come in."

Arjun followed her into the house's small sitting room. Uncle Ramesh was already there, seated in a chair that clearly served as his customary spot. He looked up as Arjun entered, his expression unreadable.

"Sit," he commanded, gesturing to a wooden chair across from him.

Arjun sat, placing a folder of documents on his lap. His hands wanted to tremble, but he forced them to remain steady.

"Six months," Uncle Ramesh said. "To the day. You're punctual, at least."

"Yes, sir."

"And you kept your word. You didn't try to contact Meera, didn't cause any problems for my family."

"I gave you my word, sir. I kept it."

Uncle Ramesh nodded slowly. "So. Tell me what you've accomplished."

Arjun opened his folder and began to lay out his documents on the low table between them—pay stubs from the factory, showing his promotion and current earnings; a letter of reference from Mr. Kapoor praising his work ethic and reliability; partnership documents with Rajan, outlining their business arrangement; bank statements showing his savings; and the title document for his motorcycle.

Uncle Ramesh examined each document carefully, his expression revealing nothing. The silence stretched out, broken only by the sound of papers being shuffled and the distant noise of the city outside.

Finally, Uncle Ramesh looked up. "You have fourteen thousand rupees in savings?"

"Fourteen thousand, eight hundred, sir. Plus my motorcycle, which is worth approximately two thousand. And I'm earning consistently now—between three and four thousand rupees per month, depending on business conditions."

"This scrap metal business," Uncle Ramesh said, tapping the partnership document. "Is it legal? You're not dealing in stolen goods?"

"Completely legal, sir," Arjun said firmly. "We buy scrap from legitimate sources—construction sites, factories, workshops—and sell to licensed smelters and recycling facilities. I can provide you with the contact information of everyone we do business with. They'll vouch for our integrity."

Uncle Ramesh was quiet again, studying Arjun with an intensity that made him acutely aware of how much hinged on this moment.

"I've made inquiries about you," Uncle Ramesh said finally. "I spoke with your supervisor at the factory. He speaks highly of you—says you're one of his most reliable workers, that you've never caused trouble, never missed a day."

Arjun's eyes widened slightly. He hadn't known Uncle Ramesh would investigate him, though perhaps he should have expected it.

"I also spoke with some people at the scrap market," Uncle Ramesh continued. "Asked about a young man named Arjun who works with old Rajan. Do you know what they told me?"

Arjun shook his head, his heart pounding.

"They said you're honest. That you don't cheat on weights or quality. That you work harder than anyone they've seen. One man told me—" Uncle Ramesh paused, and something that might have been respect flickered in his eyes, "—he told me you remind him of how people used to be. That you have old-fashioned integrity in a business where most people are looking for shortcuts."

Arjun didn't know what to say. He hadn't expected Uncle Ramesh to investigate so thoroughly, nor to hear such feedback.

"Six months ago, you were nobody," Uncle Ramesh said. "A street rat with nothing but audacity and four thousand rupees you'd somehow scraped together. Today, you sit before me with nearly fifteen thousand in savings, a legitimate job, a business partnership, and a reputation for honest work. That's... that's significant progress."

"Thank you, sir," Arjun said, hardly daring to hope.

"But," Uncle Ramesh continued, and Arjun's heart sank at that word, "earning money is only part of what makes a good husband. Meera is an educated girl. She reads, she thinks, she has ambitions beyond just keeping house. Can you offer her intellectual companionship? Growth? Opportunities?"

"I'm still learning to read and write properly, sir," Arjun admitted. "I won't pretend to be educated in the way Meera is. But I'm not afraid of learning. I'm not threatened by intelligence. And I would never hold her back from pursuing her own interests or education. If anything, I would encourage it—because Meera is the one who first taught me that knowledge has value, that the mind can be developed just like any other skill."

Uncle Ramesh leaned back in his chair, studying Arjun with an expression that was difficult to read.

"My wife thinks I'm crazy to even consider this," he said after a long moment. "She says you're still beneath our family's status, that we can do better for Meera. The clerk from Pune—he comes from a good family, has a government pension waiting, offers security and respectability."

Arjun's throat tightened, but he forced himself to speak. "I can't offer a famous family name, sir. I can't offer generational wealth or social connections. But I can offer Meera something that man might not: I can offer her a husband who will see her as a partner, not a servant. Who will value her mind and her heart. Who knows what it's like to have nothing and will therefore never take her for granted."

"Pretty words," Uncle Ramesh said. "But words are easy."

"Then judge me by my actions," Arjun said, his voice gaining strength. "Six months ago, I promised I would prove myself worthy. I worked two jobs simultaneously, slept four hours a night, took calculated risks, and saved every rupee

I could. I didn't complain. I didn't give up. I didn't take shortcuts or compromise my integrity. I did exactly what I said I would do. That's not words, sir. That's proof."

Uncle Ramesh was silent for what felt like an eternity. Then, unexpectedly, he stood up.

"Come with me," he said.

Confused but obedient, Arjun followed Uncle Ramesh out of the sitting room and up a narrow staircase to the second floor. They stopped outside a closed door.

Uncle Ramesh knocked. "Meera. Come out. There's someone here to see you."

Arjun's breath caught in his throat. He was going to see her. After six months of forced separation, of wondering and hoping and working toward this moment, he was finally going to see Meera again.

The door opened slowly, and there she was.

She looked thinner than he remembered, and there were shadows under her eyes that suggested she hadn't been sleeping well. But she was still beautiful—still the girl who had watched him from behind a broken wall, who had believed in him when no one else did.

Her eyes met his, and for a moment the world stopped. Six months of separation, of uncertainty, of hope and fear—all of it crystallized in that single look.

"Arjun," she whispered, and his name on her lips after so long felt like a benediction.

"Hello, Meera," he managed to say, his voice rough with emotion.

Uncle Ramesh watched this exchange with an inscrutable expression. Then he spoke, his voice formal and deliberate:

"Meera, this young man has come to ask, with my permission, if you would be willing to marry him. Before

I give my answer, I want to hear yours. Has he earned the right to ask? Do you want this?"

Meera's eyes filled with tears. She looked at her uncle, then back at Arjun, and when she spoke, her voice was clear and firm despite the tears.

"Yes," she said. "He's earned everything. And yes, I want this. I want him."

Uncle Ramesh nodded slowly, as though this confirmed something he'd already suspected. He turned to Arjun.

"I'm going to be honest with you. This is not the match I would have chosen for my niece. You have no family, no background, no education. By every traditional measure, you are not suitable."

Arjun's heart sank, preparing for rejection.

"But," Uncle Ramesh continued, and Arjun looked up sharply, "you have something many men with fine pedigrees lack: you have character. You have determination. You have integrity. And you have proven, beyond any doubt, that you are capable of building something from nothing through honest work and sheer willpower."

He paused, then extended his hand to Arjun. "I give my permission. You may marry Meera."

For a moment, Arjun couldn't process the words. He stared at Uncle Ramesh's outstretched hand as though it were a mirage, something that might disappear if he tried to touch it.

"Sir?" he whispered, hardly daring to believe.

"I said yes," Uncle Ramesh repeated, a slight smile touching his stern face. "Though I reserve the right to be involved in planning the wedding. And you'll be expected to treat her well—I'll be watching."

Arjun grasped Uncle Ramesh's hand, shaking it fervently, words failing him entirely. When he finally found his voice, all he could say was, "Thank you. Thank you, sir. I promise—I swear—I will spend my life proving you made the right decision."

"See that you do," Uncle Ramesh said. Then, with uncharacteristic gentleness, he added, "You have ten minutes. Talk to your bride-to-be. But keep the door open and stay where I can see you from downstairs. We may be allowing this marriage, but we still have standards of propriety."

He walked away, leaving Arjun and Meera standing in the hallway, separated by only a few feet of space that suddenly felt impossible to cross.

"Meera," Arjun said, and suddenly all the words he'd rehearsed, all the speeches he'd planned, vanished from his mind. "I—"

She crossed the distance between them and took his hands in hers, squeezing tightly. "You did it," she said, tears streaming down her face. "I knew you would. I never doubted you."

"I thought about you every day," Arjun said, his own eyes stinging. "Every moment of work, every difficulty, every time I wanted to give up—I thought of you waiting, and it kept me going."

"I was so scared," Meera admitted. "Uncle kept talking about the clerk from Pune, about how I should be practical, how I should accept what was offered. But I kept thinking: Arjun said six months. He promised. And if he says he'll do something, he'll do it."

"I would have kept working for six more months if that's what it took," Arjun said. "Six years, if necessary. However long it took to become worthy of you."

"You were always worthy," Meera said softly. "You just needed the world to see it."

They stood there, hands clasped, and in that moment Arjun felt like everything—all the suffering, all the exhaustion, all the years of invisibility and struggle—had been leading to this. To standing in a narrow hallway with the woman he loved, with a future spread out before them that they would build together.

"When I was collecting iron filings in those factory lanes," Arjun said quietly, "I never imagined I could have something like this. Someone like you. A future that wasn't just about surviving the next day."

"And when I first saw you from behind that broken wall," Meera replied, "I never imagined you would change my entire life. But you did. You showed me what determination looks like. What integrity looks like. What love looks like."

From downstairs, Uncle Ramesh's voice called up: "Time's up. We have a wedding to plan."

Arjun and Meera looked at each other and laughed—a sound of pure joy and relief.

"We should go down," Meera said, though she didn't release his hands.

"We should," Arjun agreed, also not moving.

Finally, reluctantly, they separated and walked downstairs together, not touching but close enough that their hands occasionally brushed—a promise of all the closeness to come.

CHAPTER TWELVE

The End

As Arjun left Uncle Ramesh's house an hour later, after discussions of wedding dates and ceremonies and practical arrangements, he felt like he was floating. Everything had changed. Everything was possible.

He climbed onto his motorcycle and sat there for a moment, just breathing, just absorbing the reality of what had happened.

He had done it. Against every odd, against every reasonable expectation, he had done it.

The street boy with no name, no family, no prospects—he had become someone. He had earned respect, built a life, won the right to marry the woman he loved.

As he started the motorcycle and drove through the familiar streets of the city, Arjun thought about the journey that had brought him here. The desperate days of scavenging for iron filings. The morning he had first seen Meera. The brutal months of double shifts and exhaustion. The risks taken, the lessons learned, the slow transformation from invisible to visible, from nothing to something.

And he thought about the future—the one he and Meera would build together. It wouldn't be easy. Money would sometimes be tight. Challenges would arise. But they would face them together, as partners, as equals.

He thought about the broken wall where they had first truly seen each other. It was still there, still crumbling, still marking the boundary of the industrial lane where his old life had ended and his new life had begun.

Maybe one day, he thought, he would bring his children there and tell them the story. The story of how their father had been a metal scavenger who fell in love with a girl behind a broken wall, and how that love had given him the courage to become more than anyone—including himself—had ever thought possible.

It was a good story. A true story.

And best of all, it was just beginning.

www.ingramcontent.com/pod-product-compliance
Lightning Source LLC
Chambersburg PA
CBHW031444150726
47990CB00007B/2604